D1624902

POP FLIES,
Robo-Pets, and Other Disasters

One Elm Books is an imprint of Red Chair Press LLC

Red Chair Press LLC   PO Box 333   South Egremont, MA 01258-0333

www.redchairpress.com

www.oneelmbooks.com

Publisher's Cataloging-In-Publication Data

Names: Kamata, Suzanne, 1965- author. | Bishop, Tracy, illustrator.

Title: Pop flies, robo-pets, and other disasters / Suzanne Kamata ; illustrated by Tracy Nishimura Bishop.

Description: [South Egremont, Massachusetts] : One Elm Books, an imprint of Red Chair Press LLC, [2020] | Interest age level: 009-013. | Summary: "Satoshi Matsumoto spent the last three years living in Atlanta where he was the star of his middle-school baseball team. Satoshi has a chance to be a hero at his new school in Japan until he makes a major-league error."--Provided by publisher.

Identifiers: ISBN 9781947159365 (hardcover) | ISBN 9781947159389 (ebook)

Subjects: LCSH: Baseball players--Juvenile fiction. | Teenage boys--Juvenile fiction. | New schools--Japan--Juvenile fiction. | Errors--Juvenile fiction. | CYAC: Baseball players--Fiction. | Teenage boys--Fiction. | New schools--Japan--Fiction. | Errors--Fiction.

Classification: LCC PZ7.K12668 Po 2020 (print) | LCC PZ7.K12668 (ebook) | DDC [Fic]--dc23

LC record available at https://lccn.loc.gov/2019934390

Main body text set in 12/18.5 New Century Schoolbook

Printed in Canada

819 1P S20FN

POP FLIES,
Robo-Pets, and Other Disasters

Suzanne Kamata

illustrated by Tracy Nishimura Bishop

ONE ELM
B O O K S

Egremont, Massachusetts

This book is dedicated to the baseball fans in my life –
my son, Jio; my husband, Yukiyoshi; Dad;
and in memory of my brother, Tim.

1

Only my second day of Tokushima Whirlpool Junior High School, and my bike has a flat tire. *Great.* I'm gonna be late.

I rush into the shed and dig through bamboo rakes and old plastic buckets, till I find the air pump. I open the valve, careful not to get oil on my white cuffs, and connect it to the tube of the pump. *Whoosh. Whoosh. Whoosh.* There. The tire's firm, and I don't hear any hissing. I'm good to go, but I'll have to pretend I'm in the last stretch of the Tour de France to make it on time.

Just before I'm about to take off, though, my grandpa's door slides open. He lives in a little bungalow right next to the one where Okaasan, my sister Momoko, Otosan (when he's around) and I live. Oji-chan shuffles into view, all bent and shriveled. "Satoshi, can you give me a hand?" His voice trembles.

Okaasan is one way to say 'Mom' and Otosan is a word for 'Dad' in Japanese.

I glance at our house. Okaasan's probably busy getting my sister into her leg braces, getting her teeth brushed. She goes to a school for kids with special needs where the mothers have to help all day.

"Can it wait?" I shout in Oji-chan's direction. "I've gotta go to school now."

His face crumples. *Oh, no.* I think he's about to cry.

"Are you all right?" *I gotta go. Now!* But I can't leave him like this. I park my bike and run over to his house.

"I'm okay," he says with a big sigh. "But Nana-chan isn't."

He motions me inside, where I see that Nana-chan is not barking, not scooting around with her flippers, and not blinking. In fact, she—it?—isn't moving at all. Looks like she needs to be recharged.

"I think you have to, uh, plug it in," I say, not sure if it's okay to remind him that his pet is a machine. Maybe we're supposed to act like it's a living thing.

He drops down to his knees, completely helpless.

I glance toward the door, then take a deep breath. This is going to make me late for school for sure, but I'll help him out just this once. I turn

I think you have
to plug it in.

over the robot and try to find a place to put in batteries, or to plug in a cord. Nothing. Then I go to his closet to try to find the box that it came in. The instructions are probably written on the box. Oji-chan grew up right after World War II when people didn't have much money. He saves everything. And sure enough, there is the box on the top shelf of the cupboard where he keeps his futon.

I pull it down. "World's Best Therapeutic Robo-Pet!" it says on the box. I can feel something rattling around inside. I lift the flaps and see the recharger. On one end, there's a plug. On the other, something that looks like a miniature pacifier. A pink booklet with a sketch of a baby seal on the cover—the instruction manual—is in the box, too. I flip it open to the part about juicing up the robot, and then get Nana-chan hooked up.

Oji-chan bends over her while I stick the pacifier in her mouth. It takes a few minutes, but she starts to slowly blink her eyes.

"Everything okay now?" I ask. I sneak a look at my watch. Maybe if I cut through the cemetery, I could shave off a minute or two.

"Yes. Thank you so much for helping her," he says.

For helping *you*, I think. "No problem. Well, I gotta go. See you later."

I leave him nuzzling his "pet." My back, under my polyester blazer, is all sweaty. There are hardly any other bikes out on the sidewalk. Everyone's probably already at school. I churn my legs like mad, trying to make up for lost time, but I'm still a hundred feet away from the front door when I hear the chime for first period.

I start working my feet out of my shoes before I've even reached the entrance. The backs will be all mashed down, but who cares? I stuff my sneakers into my shoe cubby and grab my indoor shoes. Then I dash down the hallway.

I slide open the door at the back of the classroom as quietly as possible and try to slip in to my desk without being noticed, but as soon as I've stepped over the threshold, Mr. Tanaka, the homeroom teacher, turns from where he's been writing on the board and looks straight at me.

"Well, Matsumoto," he says, in Japanese. "I don't know how things are at schools in America, 'Land of the Free,' but here, we have rules. I expect you to be in your seat when the bell rings, no matter who your grandfather is."

I know that a guy like Mr. Tanaka isn't interested in hearing my excuses for being late. "I'm sorry, sir," I say. "It won't happen again."

He stares at me for a moment longer. "Since you were late, you will copy the first page in the textbook three times," he says, then goes back to writing on the board.

That's just terrific. What a waste of time.

The big-eyed brown-haired girl who sits next to me—Misa, I think her name is—gives me a sideways glance. Am I imagining it, or does she look sympathetic? I roll my eyes, and she cracks a smile and then turns back to the front.

"Next period we will have a visit from Jerry, the new assistant English teacher from America," Mr. Tanaka announces, rocking back on his heels.

A buzz starts up at the back of the room. I catch a few words: "last year surfer played the guitar." One girl actually squeals. They probably think they'll be meeting a guy who looks like a movie star. Little do they know; most Americans are pretty normal looking. Some are even ugly.

"And don't forget," Mr. Tanaka adds. "The day after tomorrow, there will be a test."

What? Already? This cannot be happening to

me. My throat goes dry and my stomach flips. I wish I could get up and run straight out the door and never come back. A flapping sound fills the room as notebooks open. Just about everyone scrawls down a reminder. For me, it's as if a hairy beast with yellow eyes and fangs is suddenly looming over me. There's no need to make a note about the big date because it'll be impossible for me to forget. The test will probably be filled with kanji, even though this is supposedly English class. I'll fail for sure, and then I won't be able to play baseball.

2

During the break between Home Room and first period, I stay at my desk and stare straight ahead, trying to teleport myself back to my school in Atlanta. What I wouldn't give to see those walls slathered with posters of NBA stars telling us to R-E-A-D and the kids practicing hip hop dance in the hallway and the writing teacher with her cornrows in clackety beads! These white walls are bor-i-n-g. A lump forms in my throat. I'm suddenly homesick, even though this is supposed to be home. My dad is no longer on overseas assignment for the robotics company that puts rice on our table. Now he's been transferred to Tokyo, and we're left to fend for ourselves. I can feel my eyeballs start to burn and everything starts to get a little blurry. Oh, no!

The bell rings. I close my eyes and shake my

head, get myself together. Showtime. I look over at Misa. Her face is blank. She doesn't look excited at all about meeting an American.

Mr. Tanaka comes in about five minutes later. He's alone.

"Where's Mr. Jerry?" a girl in the back calls out.

"He will be here soon," Mr. Tanaka says. "He had to use the restroom."

The classroom becomes silent as we sit there waiting. Finally, we hear slippers scuffing down the hallway. The door to the classroom slides open and in comes a guy who looks to be twice as big as our English teacher. He's huffing as if he's just climbed Mt. Fuji. His stomach oozes over the top of his khaki pants. He looks like he hasn't worked out a day in his life. Not only that, but his wispy blond hair is starting to recede and his face is all blotchy. He is not what you would call "hot" or even "cool."

I swear I can feel the energy leaving the room. The girls seem to deflate.

"Okay, let's begin," Mr. Tanaka says.

The class leader orders us to stand and bow. After we're back in our seats, Mr. Tanaka moves to the side of the classroom and holds his hand palm up to Jerry. "Please go ahead," he says.

For a moment, Jerry just stands there, staring into our faces, as if he isn't sure what he's supposed to do.

And then I hear Shintaro Nakamoto whispering with some other boys in the back. My shoulders tense. Shintaro and I played on the same baseball team in elementary school. We weren't exactly friends, though. In a flash, it all comes back to me: the crunch of that cicada in my mouth, the mounds of dog poop in my sneakers, the ice cubes down the front of my briefs.

Now, Shintaro says, "Look! He's wearing the toilet slippers!" There's a pause as we all take in the green vinyl slippers, no doubt splattered with pee, and then the whole class erupts into laughter.

"*Kitanai!*" one girl says. Gross!

It takes a moment for Jerry to figure out why everyone is laughing. My skin prickles. I remember how my classmates in Atlanta made fun of me when I peeled my grapes before eating them, or when I used a ruler to draw a straight line. I never knew what I was doing to make people laugh.

Finally, Mr. Tanaka explains. "Mr. Jerry, you have forgotten your room slippers. It's best to not

wear the toilet slippers in the classroom."

Jerry's entire head flushes. "Uh, excuse me for a moment." He shuffles quickly to the door and goes off to correct his mistake. Mr. Tanaka smirks. I wonder if he is thinking about how superior he is to the American English teacher.

When Jerry comes back, wearing cloth slippers in a blue and red plaid, his heels hanging over the edges, Mr. Tanaka sits down behind his desk in the corner, and nods to Jerry. "Please go ahead," he says again. I wonder if he is standing aside on purpose, waiting for Jerry to fail somehow.

"Okay, then," Jerry says, still flustered. "I guess I'll tell you a little bit about myself."

He writes his name—Jerry Fisher—and then he draws a map on the blackboard. He is from South Dakota, not California or New York or Hawaii. In other words, he's not from any place my classmates have ever heard of or would want to visit. I can almost hear their brains click off. To my left, another student is quietly studying a list of vocabulary words. One of the girls in the back is braiding her bangs.

When Jerry has finished telling us about the corn palace and the Badlands, he asks us if there is anything else we would like to know about him. There are still thirty minutes of class time remaining.

Silence. Everyone looks down at their desks, including me.

"Mr. Matsumoto," Mr. Tanaka says from behind his desk. "Why don't you ask Mr. Jerry a question?"

I look up. Sweat has soaked through Jerry's shirt. There are big dark blotches at his armpits.

"Mr. Matsumoto lived in the United States for three years," Mr. Tanaka explains to Jerry.

"Cool!" Jerry says, his face suddenly alight. His gaze skitters around as he tries to locate me.

"Mr. Matsumoto, please stand up and ask your question!" Mr. Tanaka says.

I can't think of anything to say. He's already told us about his family (two brothers, two sisters), his pet (a St. Bernard) and his hobby (wood-carving). He's told us more than we'd ever want to know about South Dakota. Should I ask him a sports question? He doesn't look very athletic, but maybe he's a Twins fan.

"Do you like baseball?" I ask. It's a simple question that everyone can understand. I don't want to be a show off.

"Do I like baseball?" Jerry says. "I love it! I live for opening day." His enthusiasm is a little alarming. For a moment, I'm afraid he's going to come over and hug me. Better to cut him off before he gets carried away, I think. He's already lost the rest of the class with his native-speaker English.

"Thanks," I mutter, and sit back down. I'll do anything to get the spotlight off of me.

He looks a little disappointed, as if he wasn't finished talking, as if he wanted to tell us about his favorite teams, his favorite players, his all-time favorite plays, but then a hand shoots up at the back of the room.

"Yes?"

Shintaro scoots his chair back and stands up, a smirk on his face. I notice that his eyebrows have been razored into thin lines. "Do you have a lover?" he asks.

Jerry seems to shrink back into himself. His face goes all red again. "Uh, not really. No." He clears his throat. "I don't have a girlfriend."

Nobody would have ever asked something like that at my school in the States. I can't believe Mr. Tanaka is sitting behind his desk giggling along with the rest of the class. I doubt that Mr. Tanaka has a girlfriend, either. Who'd go out with that guy? Not that I'm some kind of expert, but there were a couple of girls at my school in Atlanta who wrote notes to me.

At any rate, for better or worse, Shintaro has broken the ice. Several other students work up the nerve to ask questions after that. We find out that Jerry's favorite color is blue, that he doesn't play sports, and that he likes to do Sudoku puzzles in his spare time. Somehow, the hour crawls by, and then the chime rings, setting Jerry—and the rest of us—free.

But the thing is, he doesn't flee. Not right away. He takes a few steps toward me. "So, Satoshi," he says, "where did you live in the States?"

The other students keep their distance. I imagine thought bubbles over their heads containing the words "brown noser," "teacher's pet," "Mr. Jerry's special friend." No way am I racking up popularity points by being seen with the foreign teacher. As they make their way to the door, past Jerry, they avoid eye contact.

"Atlanta," I say.

"Oh, cool," Jerry says, coming even closer. "Home of the Braves, right? Hank Aaron and all that." He seems really eager to talk, and I wonder how long it's been since he's had the chance to speak English to someone who can actually understand him.

We're a little island at the center of the classroom. I want to jump into the water. "So, uh, nice class," I say, feinting to the right. "See you later."

His smile fades. "Yeah, see you, Satoshi. Hey, maybe you can help me..."

Oh, no. Is he going to ask me to be his assistant or something? I pretend I don't hear. I hurry out of the room, and move on to P.E.

3

After school, I put on my practice uniform and join the other baseball players on the field.

Coach Ogawa is there, standing by the fence with Shintaro Nakamoto.

I creep up behind, essay in hand.

Yesterday, at the first team meeting, Coach gathered us all together and said, "Before we get started, I'd like you to give some thought to why you want to play baseball for Tokushima Whirlpool Junior High School. What made you choose this game in the first place? And what are your goals as a player on this team? Think about these questions, and then go home and write me an essay in reply. Bring it to the field tomorrow when we have our first official practice."

Riding home alone on my bicycle, I started thinking about the question. I don't get what writing has to do with baseball, but if I wanted to play on the team, I had to come up with something. So, what made me choose baseball? I'm not sure how to answer that one. I've loved the game for as long as I can remember.

My buddy Rico would have the perfect story to tell if he were here. He once told me that he originally thought he was destined to be a soccer god like Maradona or Messi. He spent all of his free time kicking a ball, or bouncing it on his knee, off his head. He even practiced in the house. Nobody in his family cared when he knocked over a lamp with the soccer ball because they all believed he was destined for greatness. Then one day, he was out in his driveway, working on his dribbling, and he saw a fresh oil stain from his father's drippy car.

"It wasn't just any oil spill," Rico told me. "It was the face of Roberto Clemente."

Rico's family is Catholic. They believe in signs and miracles, and this, Rico realized, was a sign. He immediately kicked aside his soccer ball and switched to baseball. By the time I met him, in a middle school in Atlanta, he had become a neighborhood star.

I wish I had a story like Rico's to write down,

but I don't. I never played soccer, never had any sort of lightning bolt moment. My earliest memory is of me, standing in the front of the TV with my plastic bat, trying to time my swings with the hurls of the pro pitcher on the screen. I remember a voice in the background saying, "Nice one! Good timing!" The voice of Oji-chan.

My grandfather—*Oji-chan*—is the one who taught me how to play. He played baseball himself, up until he was my age. He was the pitcher for Tokushima Shogyo, a vocational high school, where he was studying to be a secretary or a clerk, some nice office job. Even back then, Tokusho's team was really strong.

It was Oji-chan's dream to play in the National High School Baseball Tournament sponsored by the Asahi newspaper at Koshien. But then war broke out. The tournament was suspended. Another competition was held instead. It was called the "Promote the Fighting Spirit Tournament." Only sixteen teams took part, not the usual twenty-three, and the event wasn't sponsored by the Asahi, but it was held at Koshien Stadium. Oji-chan pitched his team to the prefectural championship, and then on to Koshien where they won the whole tournament.

I've seen old, yellowed photos of him with his hair buzzed down to his scalp, a Japanese kanji character on his uniform instead of a number. He looks really happy in that picture, but he always says that it didn't count because it wasn't the official tournament. Tokusho didn't go into the record books as a Koshien champion. Plus, they were criticized for playing a game created by the dreaded Americans, the enemy. The next year, Oji-chan had to quit high school to work in a munitions factory. The tournament didn't start up again until after the war was over, and by then it was too late for him.

After the war was over, he went back to school, became a teacher, and started his own school, Peace Junior High School. He's not in charge of the school anymore, though. My dad didn't want to take it over, so it's out of the family. There's a new guy, and a new name—Tokushima Whirlpool Junior High School, named after the giant natural whirlpools churning in the nearby straits of Naruto.

Now I step up to Coach and Shintaro, and catch the end of their conversation. "Go get a haircut, Nakamoto."

In addition to the shaved eyebrows, his hair

is all wavy and layered down to his collar. He looks more like the member of a boy band than a baseball player. He takes a step back and bumps into me.

"Hey, watch it!" he says, as if I'd stumbled into him and not the other way around.

"Sorry." I can still feel his fingernails tearing through my skin and that bug in my mouth from years ago.

Shintaro snarls something under his breath about the haircut requirement being a violation of his rights as a human being, and shoves past me out to the field.

As soon as he's away from me, I feel my shoulders loosen up. I let out the breath I've been holding and present my essay with two hands and a slight bow.

Coach Ogawa skims over my words, and nods. "Good. Go run some laps."

"Yes, sir!" I turn away, but he calls me back.

"You could use a haircut, too."

My hair isn't all long and girly like Shintaro's, but it's not exactly a *bozu*. I don't mind getting it cut, though. "Yes, sir!" I say.

Out on the field, I do a few hamstring stretches, then join the others in a slow jog around the perimeter.

I'm moving my legs, breathing in, breathing out. Minding my own business. Suddenly, Shintaro comes up beside me. He matches my stride.

I try to keep my eyes ahead, try to ignore him,

but his elbow crashes into mine.

"Ow!"

"Hey, America," he says.

My feet pound the ground. Left, right, left.

"Hey, I'm talking to you."

Okay, okay. He's not going to go away unless I listen. "What?"

"Don't think you're some kind of prince because of your grandpa," he sneers.

"I don't." I'd rather not talk to him at all, but here's the thing. His father owns a nightclub where the customers have dragons tattooed across their shoulders and hacked off fingers. According to legend, they drink liquor made with snake venom, the vipers themselves coiled at the bottom of the bottles. I try to imagine standing up to him, but all I get is an image of Shintaro's dad cutting off my finger, which is what gangsters do to people who are disloyal. Just the thought of it makes me want to hurl.

"Just so you know your place," Shintaro says, before sprinting ahead of me.

I study my shoes, remembering that time in Atlanta when I walked out of my ESL class and a big kid in chains and a backwards baseball cap slammed me against my locker.

"Hey, you speak-ee English-ee?," he said, his spit showering my face.

Please hit me in the stomach, I thought. Anywhere but the face. Anywhere that won't bleed.

Jamal came to my rescue. "Leave my friend alone," he said. "He's our homerun king."

Back here in Japan there's no one to stick up for me, to protect me from bullies. "Sometimes you have to go along to get along," one of my teachers in America used to say. I guess I need to try to be Shintaro's friend, or at least try not to make him mad. But I avoid him for the rest of practice.

We play catch, take a thousand swings of the bat, practice fielding and base-running and batting, and then finally, we scrimmage.

Kikawa, the third-year ace pitcher is tossing the balls. He's got a wicked slider, but I think I can handle him. On my first turn, I wallop the ball deep into left field. On my second, I drive it through the hole between first and second base. My ball goes farther and faster than anyone else's. No one says anything as we pack up the gear after practice, but I'm sure they've noticed.

4

At lunchtime the next day, I decide I'd rather eat alone but then I hear Shintaro's big voice. "Hey Matsumoto, baseball players eat together. Get over here." So I drag my desk across the room and nudge it up against Junji's and Shintaro's. We are the only guys in this class who are on the team.

They've already started in on their bentos.

"So what's the story about that girl?" I ask in a low voice, jerking my head toward Misa. She's eating by herself. I feel sorry for her.

"We don't talk to her," Shintaro says. "She's not one of us."

The "us" gives me a surge of joy. For the first time since I got back, I feel included. But I know it's wrong to leave others out. "What do you mean?" I ask.

"She's *hafu*," Junji says.

"Half what?"

"Her mom's American, I guess," Shintaro says, not bothering to lower his voice.

So that explains her brown hair and light eyes. I knew there was something different about the way she looked, but I couldn't quite figure it out. There were never any mixed-race kids around here when I was growing up.

"I've seen her mom before," Shintaro says. "She's big and loud."

I can't help but cringe. In Atlanta, my own mother always seemed so tiny and quiet, like a mouse. I was embarrassed because she seemed like a little kid compared to my friends' mothers. I wonder what Shintaro would say about my sister with her flailing arms, and Oji-chan with his pet robot.

Shintaro and Junji suddenly remember that I'm just back from America and they start battering me with questions.

"Is it true that most Americans are fat like pigs?"

"Did you really have three months off during summer vacation? And no cram school?"

"Do all Americans have guns like we see on TV?"

I try to answer their questions as best as I can. Just as suddenly, they lose interest and move on to another topic.

I glance over at Misa, wondering if she heard the guys talking about her. She seems to have curled more tightly around her lunch, like a turtle trying to get back into its shell.

• • •

By the end of the school day, I have a list of stuff that I need to buy: watercolors for Art, notebooks for English and Japanese, batting gloves and a generic practice uniform for baseball. When I get home, I hand it over to my mother.

"Could you give me some money?" I ask, thinking I'll go to the mall by myself.

"Why don't we all go together?" she says. "Momoko needs some things, too, and we can go to the food court after we finish shopping."

"Well, okay." I was hoping to play some video games and read magazines in the bookstore, but it's her wallet. And there's this pizza place in the food court. I haven't had pizza since we were in the States.

It takes a while for everyone to get into the car. I pop over and tell Oji-chan that we're going out while Okaasan helps Momoko put on her leg braces. Then, my mother wheels my sister out to the car, supports her while she climbs into the seat and collapses the wheelchair.

"I'll do that," I say, stepping in to lift the wheelchair into the trunk.

When we get to the Dream Town Mall, we have to do everything in reverse: unload and unfold the chair, help Momoko out of the car and into the wheelchair, and buckle her in.

"Why don't we split up?" I say once we're inside. "I'll go to the sporting goods store and you can pick up the other stuff." To be totally honest, I don't want anyone to see me shopping with my mother. I mean really, how uncool is that?

She hesitates for a moment, but then hands over some money. "Okay. Meet us at the food court in thirty minutes."

"Thanks!" I dash off in the direction of the sporting goods store.

This mall is a lot like American malls, except for the stores. Of course this one has a Starbucks and Zara, but there's also a sushi restaurant and a shop that sells kimonos and boutiques with crazy English names like Room Next, Opaque Clip, and Starvations.

Xebio Sports is at the end of the mall. I have to go past racks of jogging and golf gear and swimsuits to get to the baseball department. I'm thumbing through piles of white baseball practice shirts when I hear my name.

I turn and look. "Oh, hey, Junji."

He's with his mom, a short woman with glasses

and long hair. Her arms are piled with work-out clothes.

"You here alone?" he asks.

"Uh, my mom's here, too." Junji doesn't know about my sister. No one does. She was still pretty much a baby when we left for Atlanta. No one would have expected her to be walking back then anyhow.

For a second, I have this wild fear that Junji's mom will want to talk to mine. About what, I don't know, but it's a huge relief when he turns to go. "Well, I guess we're done here. See you at practice tomorrow."

"Yeah, bye!"

I find what I need and take it up to the cash register after I'm sure that they're gone. A glance at the clock on the wall tells me that I still have a few more minutes before I have to meet Okaasan and Momoko, so I stop off in the bookstore for a quick flip through a magazine about pro baseball.

When I get to the food court, I see Okaasan and Momoko sitting at a table with a foreign woman with butter-colored hair. Right next to her is Misa, the *hafu* girl from my class. The one Shintaro says not to talk to.

Misa and Momoko are exchanging notes on a

pad of paper. Looks like they've already bonded.

Okaasan looks up. "Find everything you need?" Her cheeks are flushed, like they get when she's happy or excited.

"Yeah." I nod at Misa. She smiles back.

"I just met your friend, here, and her mother," Okaasan says. "They're going to eat with us."

"Super." I look over my shoulder, making sure that Junji isn't around. The coast is clear for now, at least.

"Get some food. Have anything you want!" Okaasan gestures to the vendors lining the square selling everything from ramen noodles to spinach smoothies to pizza. She hands me her wallet and points to the hand-held buzzer. "We've already ordered."

Since she's being so generous, I hit up three different restaurant booths. I'm in the mood for a burger, pizza, *and* noodles. I go back to the table with a buzzer from each place.

Okaasan and Misa's mother are talking about English.

"It's so great she finally has someone to speak it with," Misa's mom says. "Someone besides me, I mean."

"Well, Jerry comes to our school. You know, the

American guy," Misa says.

Wow. She's suddenly totally fluent. I've heard her say a few words in class, but she always speaks with a heavy Japanese accent.

"You sound American," I blurt out.

"Well, I *am*," she says. "I have an American passport."

"Then why do you pretend to have a Japanese accent in class?"

Her mother looks surprised. "You do?"

She shifts uncomfortably. "I'm trying to blend in."

Like that's going to happen. But I know what she means. I'm getting picked on enough myself.

Okaasan starts going on about how happy she is to have found someone from America living in our town, and how it'll be good for my English as well. And then before I know what's happening, she's inviting Misa and her family over for dinner.

I imagine Misa blabbing all over town about visiting my house and meeting my disabled sister and confused grandfather. And will I have to talk to her at school now? This can't be happening.

All three buzzers start going off at once, but I've just lost my appetite.

5

The next afternoon I bike to a barber shop. When I go through the door, a little bell tinkles. There's an older guy in one chair, all lathered up, and another guy wearing a white smock, waving a straight razor around while he tells some story. At the sound of the bell, they become silent and look my way.

"Hi, there. What can I do for you?" the barber asks.

"Um, give me a *bozu*," I say.

"Have a seat." He juts his chin toward a row of chairs by the window.

I take one, keeping my eyes averted as he resumes shaving. If he nicks the guy, I don't want to see. One drop of blood and I'll be down on the floor, with the hair clippings.

"What team you play for?" the guy in the chair asks.

Um, give me a bozu.

I almost say "The Bobcats," but then I catch myself. "Tokushima Whirlpool Junior High."

The barber sucks in air through his teeth. "It's been awhile since they won a tournament, hasn't it? I heard that this might be the last year for baseball over there. If they don't make it to the finals, then it'll be all over. Enrollment is down and they're looking for ways to bring in new students."

"That new owner is a businessman," the guy in the chair says. "Heard he wants to do away with baseball and bring in some new-fangled sports like lacrosse and ribbon twirling."

The barber chuckles. "You mean rhythmic gymnastics?"

"Yeah, whatever. With the hoops and all."

What? They carry on this way for awhile, but my mind is stuck on the baseball part. Do away with it just because the team hasn't won a tournament in awhile? First thing I heard about this.

"So what position do you play?" the barber asks me.

"Right field," I say.

"You're going to be another Ichiro, huh?" the barber asks.

The guy in the chair laughs and slaps his knee.

Hey, I can hit the ball. You don't have to laugh at me. "I'll do my best," I say.

Then the barber starts talking about Ichiro and Hideki Matsui and Yu Darvish, about how all the best players are leaving Japan, and don't they have any sense of loyalty? The guy in the chair has to keep still, or else he might get cut with the razor. He doesn't say anything, just hums a little in agreement.

I don't hum anything. I think about what will happen if we don't win a championship or at least make it to the finals. If I can't play baseball in junior high, I won't be able to get onto a high school team. And if I can't get onto a high school team, there's no way I'll ever be able to play in college or go pro. And Oji-chan. He would be crushed. Suddenly my stomach is going in circles and there's a big lump in my throat.

When it's my turn, I settle into the leather chair. It's still warm from the other guy. The barber clips a plastic cape around my neck. He pats my cheek and chuckles. "I guess you don't need a shave yet, do you?"

"No, sir."

"Well, then," he says, and looks at me in the mirror. My hair isn't all that long. It's above my ears, respectable by most standards, but it's not a bozu—not the haircut of Buddhist priests, soldiers, and those who are truly devoted to baseball. "Ready?" he asks.

"Yes."

He grabs an electric shaver from a tray beside the chair and starts at the back of my neck. The vibrations tickle. I watch in the mirror as he mows down row after row of hair, until there's almost nothing left. Black clippings flutter onto the cape.

6

Maybe those guys in the barber shop were wrong. I tell myself this for the rest of the weekend. I mean, how can the school even think about doing away with the baseball team? Okay, so I know that a lot of the baseball players are there on scholarships, which means they aren't paying tuition. And the less popular a sport is, the easier it is to make it to a national competition. If Tokushima Whirlpool Junior High has the only lacrosse team in the prefecture, they'll be local champs by default. They'll have a chance at winning a trophy in Tokyo or abroad. That would bring glory to the school, and maybe more students and more money. Somehow, I have to figure out what's going on. Maybe Junji knows something. Or Shintaro.

Monday, when I walk into English class, everyone starts laughing, and I forget about my quest. I stop in my tracks and look around, trying to find out what's so funny. My hair isn't sticking up, my fly isn't open, but it's obvious that they are laughing at me.

"He's like a foreigner!" Shintaro says.

Mr. Tanaka smirks, but he doesn't bother to clue me in.

And then a kid in the front row points to my feet.

I look down. Uh-oh. *The toilet slippers.* My face is on fire as I back out of the classroom to retrieve my shoes from the bathroom. In Atlanta, everybody wore the same shoes all day, except for P.E. and baseball. In our house, I go around in my socks. It's easy to forget to change shoes, but my classmates seem to be on the look-out for the ways in which I'm different now.

When I get back to the classroom, everyone has sobered up. Mr. Tanaka is standing at the front with the corrected tests that we took last week.

• • •

"I will return the tests in order of ranking—worst to first," he says. He holds up a sheaf of papers stapled together. "Nakamoto Shintaro."

Over the weekend, Shintaro got a haircut, too. You can see his neck now, though he didn't get a *bozu*.

Now, he swaggers to the front of the class, snatches his test out of the teacher's hand, and struts back to his desk. He takes one look at the score, crumples the paper, and shoves it behind some books.

I try to keep my mind off Shintaro by staring at Misa's head. Luckily, she hasn't tried to talk to me at school. She stays in her chair until almost the entire class has gotten their test scores back. Junji goes up, and then those girls in the corner who all look alike. They probably all got the same score because they shared answers. Finally, Mr. Tanaka calls Misa's name. The girls cut their eyes at her and talk to each other behind cupped hands. When she sits back down, I lean forward and see that she got a big fat 90. Good for her.

"Matsumoto Satoshi." He says my name as if it makes his mouth hurt.

I go up and get my paper—92. I feel like punching the air, but then I catch Shintaro looking at me as if he's a tiger and I'm some tiny rodent. I plaster my poker face on and slouch back to my seat.

• • •

At the start of baseball practice, Shintaro hands over his essay. Coach reads a few lines, grunts and nods, and waves Shintaro off to the field.

Now's my chance to have a word with the coach. I step up to him and clear my throat.

"Yes?"

"Uh, sorry to bother you, but I heard a rumor in the barber shop. I wondered if it might be true."

He scowls. "And what rumor might that be?"

"Well, sir, I heard that if our team doesn't make it to the finals in one of the tournaments this year, the baseball team will be eliminated."

A dozen emotions float across his face— surprise, anger, sadness. "That may be true," he says in a low voice, "but keep it to yourself. If that rumor gets out, we won't get any decent new players next year, will we? Besides, we're going to win a tournament this year. Got that?"

"Yes, sir." I bow, doff my cap, and run out to the infield. I can't help thinking that my teammates would all try harder if they knew the truth, but then again, maybe they'd cave under pressure, or transfer to other schools. I try not to think about what I've learned as we smooth out the dirt field with wooden rakes.

By the time we're done raking, I've already worked up a sweat. The other guys are setting up the netting for batting practice, and hauling out bins of balls and bats wrapped in canvas.

Someone pulls up in a car and gets out—some guy who's come to see the coach, maybe a rep from a sporting goods store. The players near the edge of the field stop in their tracks, doff their caps, and bow to him, saying, *"Konnichiwa!"* This is what we're supposed to do every time we have a "visitor."

When everything's all prepped, we start running laps around the edge of the field.

"Okay, guys. Pair up for catch!" the team captain yells out.

"You wanna play with me?" Junji asks.

"Sure."

We get a nice rhythm going, the ball volleying back and forth between us, so that I hardly notice when another visitor comes by. Out of the corner of my eye, I see some of my teammates pause and bow, hear them shout out a greeting—*"Konnichiwa!"*— but I'm just thinking about the ball coming toward me. It smacks into my mitt. I grab it with my other hand, pull back my arm for the throw, and fire it to Junji.

But this time, he doesn't raise his arm, doesn't even try to catch the ball. It shoots over his shoulder and crashes into the dirt behind him. Junji's not looking at me, or the ball. His attention is off to the side, where the visitor is.

I scowl at him. How can we have a decent team if no one takes practice seriously? But then Junji points toward the fence and says, "Satoshi, isn't that..."

I shield my eyes from the sun and look over to where he's pointing. Coach is talking to someone. Not the guy from the sporting goods store, but another man, a smaller man who looks like he's stooping. He looks somehow familiar, but it takes another second before my stomach goes all cold and I realize who it is.

"My grandfather," I say, finishing Junji's sentence. *What is he doing here?* "Excuse me for a second," I say. Junji nods and I dash over to the fence.

Coach Ogawa is talking to Oji-chan. He's smiling and nodding, as if they know each other. Some of the other players glance over at me as I

walk up to them. As I jog past Shintaro, I hear him say, "crazy old man," just loud enough for me to hear.

I suddenly feel like a volcano, about to erupt. Keep those feet moving, Matsumoto, I tell myself. Don't throw your mitt at him. Just ignore him. Pretend he's not even there.

Oji-chan is wearing a long-sleeved white T-shirt with a big brown stain on the front, and sweatpants, but they're on backwards. And on his feet, he's got on the same sandals that he wears to shuffle around in the yard. I look around for a bicycle, or even a car that he might have used to get here, but there's nothing. He must have come on foot. It would take someone like me about half an hour to walk here from our house. For him, maybe an hour.

I catch Coach Ogawa's eye, take my cap off and bow. "I'm so sorry about this. He's my grandfather. I'll take him home."

"Satoshi-kun," Oji-chan says. "I thought you boys might be hungry." He holds up a plastic bag of dried persimmons. There's hardly enough for the entire team, and besides, the managers will be making rice balls for everyone, but Coach Ogawa thanks him and takes the bag. Then he steps away to give us some privacy.

"Does anyone know you're here? Okaasan?"

He scrunches up his face. "I don't know where your mother is."

"Wait here," I say. I go into the clubhouse where I've stashed my gear and dig my cell phone out of my bag. I try calling my house, but no one answers. And then I dial Okaasan's number. Still nothing. I could send him home on my bicycle, but I'm not sure that he wouldn't get lost. And I could ask someone— Coach Ogawa, maybe—to drive him home, but then I would be indebted to him. My parents wouldn't like that. And I don't have any money to call a cab. I guess I'll have to walk him home.

I gather up my stuff and tell Coach Ogawa that I'm leaving.

"Okay," he says. "See you tomorrow."

I'm a little surprised he's being so nice about this, but I'm grateful. "Thank you, sir."

Oji-chan is still waiting by the fence. We walk to where my bicycle is parked, and I look at his sandals. "Why don't you take the bike?" I say. "I'll walk along behind."

His feet must be hurting, because he doesn't object.

7

It takes forty-five minutes to get back to the house. Oji-chan's going slowly so that I can keep up, or maybe because his legs are tired from walking. The bike wobbles a little, but he doesn't fall down. I jog alongside him, my eyes on the sidewalk. Meanwhile, Oji-chan greets every single person we come across—a granny out for a walk with a baby strapped to her back, some kids squatting by the side of the road poking in the grass with sticks, a middle-aged couple out for their exercise. Some of them greet him back, some, like the kids, just look at him.

When we get home, I find that his front door is unlocked. I slide open the door and hear a "yip yip!" Nana-chan appears in the entryway.

Oji-chan leans down and strokes her fur. "That's a good girl," he says.

I roll my eyes. I could just leave them alone together and go back to practice. Oji-chan doesn't look too lonely with the seal there, but I'm not sure that I can trust him to stay put. I'd better keep him company until Okaasan and Momoko get home. An idea pops into my head.

"Wait here," I say.

He's still murmuring to Nana-chan, but he nods as if he's heard me.

I go across the yard and let myself into our house, run upstairs and grab a shoebox from under my bed. It's full of baseball cards. I collected them when I was in elementary school, and Oji-chan and I used to quiz each other about the players. He might like doing that now, I think. It might help him to remember.

I change out of my uniform and then take the box down to Oji-chan's house. He's sitting on a cushion at the table, Nana-chan at his side.

"Are you thirsty?" I ask him. He must be, since he walked all that way, and then rode back on the bicycle. Without waiting for an answer, I pour us each a glass of tea, drop in some ice cubes, and then join him at the table.

"Oji-chan, remember these cards?" I lift the lid

of the box and show him the little stacks, divided by team and secured by rubber bands.

He nods vaguely.

"Guess who this is." I pull out a card. "He played for the Yomiuri Giants. He hit 868 home runs in his career, making him Japan's home run king."

A smile crinkles his face. "That's easy. Oh Sadaharu."

Phew. In spite of his dirty clothes and his surprise visit to school, he's basically himself today.

"Okay, here's another one. He was a pitcher for the Giants. He struck out Babe Ruth and Lou Gehrig."

It takes a minute for him to respond to this one, but he gets it right: "Sawamura Eiji."

We're on about the tenth card, and Oji-chan's 8 for 9, when the door slides open and Okaasan appears. *"Tadaima!"* she says. "I'm home!"

Her mouth makes an O when she sees me. "What are you doing here?" she asks. "Don't you have practice?"

I explain to her about what happened.

"I thought he'd be okay by himself for a little while," she says, shaking her head. "I guess I was wrong. We're going to have to keep a better eye on him, or else..."

"Don't even say it," I plead. "We can handle this. I can."

Oji-chan is not some helpless old man destined to be slouched in a chair in the day room of a nursing home. He is a former star slugger! A superhero teacher! The founder of Peace School a.k.a. Whirlpool Junior High School! He is the man who taught me everything I know about baseball, and I know that there is more inside his head that he will eventually share, when he's feeling on top of things. This might be a bad patch, but we'll get through it. I'm not going to let him down.

8

At breakfast the next morning Okaasan says, "He's gotten worse. Maybe we should think about alternatives."

"Like what?" I ask, sliding into my seat across from Momoko who's already eaten half of her grilled salmon.

"Well, he might be better off in a group home where people can look after him twenty-four hours a day."

Okaasan scoops rice out of the steamer and puts a bowl of it in front of me.

"He would hate that," I say. I remember visiting my great-grandmother in a nursing home when I was a little kid. The place smelled like pee and cleaning chemicals. There were no carpets or tatami anywhere, only scuffed linoleum, and the walls were painted puke green. I remember lots of moaning and shouting. It was scary. Not only would Oji-chan be miserable, but he wouldn't be able to go to my games.

"We could get him shoes with GPS trackers. You know, like little kids wear sometimes."

Just then, Momoko's left hand suddenly jerks, knocking over her glass of tea. The spill spreads to the edge of the table, falling into her lap. She starts wailing loudly.

Okaasan rushes over with a towel.

"Or, we could just try to spend more time with him," I say trying to continue the conversation.

"Would you be willing to quit baseball?" Okaasan asks, sopping up tea and refilling Momoko's glass.

I gulp. I hadn't thought it would come to that, but what can I say? I'm supposed to be the man of the house, after all. "Yeah, I guess." My voice is barely a whisper.

9

I manage to make it to school on time for once. In English class, Mr. Tanaka asks us to read an essay in our textbooks. It's about global warming, and although there are a few words that I have to look up, I get through it quickly. The others are still reading when I look up from the text. I can hear the clickety clack of forty students looking up words on their electronic dictionaries.

After about ten minutes, Mr. Tanaka asks Junji to read the first paragraph out loud. Poor kid, his accent is worse than our teacher's, and he seems to stumble over every fifth word. His face is as red as a pickled plum. I feel kind of sorry for him. When his turn is over, my shoulders loosen.

Misa reads the next paragraph. She's still putting on the phony accent. She struggles with one word and I can't help thinking that that's fake, too. Another girl who sits toward the back reads next, followed by a boy with glasses a couple rows over until the entire essay has been read out loud.

"And now, we will translate this essay. Who can change the first sentence into Japanese?"

Oh, brother. This has to be the dullest class ever. I can hardly keep my eyes open. I slide my Japanese book out of my desk, and take a look at the new kanji I'm supposed to remember. I practice writing them in the margins of my English book. Soon the white spaces are full of pencil strokes.

" Matsumoto!"

I look up to see the entire class staring at me. Mr. Tanaka, too. "Do you think just because you got a good score on the English test that you don't need to listen? You still have plenty to learn, young man. You are not as smart as you think you are."

"Whatever," I say under my breath.

"Pardon me?" He moves closer to me, his eyeballs bulging.

And then it's as if all of the things that I have to get used to again, every rude comment about my time away, turns into a tornado of anger. It starts in my stomach, and then it works its way through my chest, to my throat. I'm sick of this guy picking on me. Shintaro was late this morning, but Mr. Tanaka didn't yell at him in front of everyone, didn't give him extra homework. I'm not really behaving all that differently from anyone else in this classroom, and yet he always singles me out.

I stand up so that we are face to face. My hands curl into fists, and my face feels like it's on fire. English gushes out of me. "Why are you always picking on me? Why do you have to give me such a hard time? I'm just minding my own business, trying to get used to this place again. I don't know what your deal is. Why can't you leave me alone?"

The classroom is totally silent. Some of the students look a little scared. Of me? Or of what Mr. Tanaka will do next? Shintaro is smirking. Misa looks curious.

Mr. Tanaka's face is now purple. I'm pretty sure he didn't understand a word I said, and it's probably killing him.

"You will copy this page ten times!" he shrieks, pointing to the textbook with a trembling finger. "I don't want to see your face or hear your voice for the rest of the class!"

I could protest, but what good would that do?

He might report me to Coach Ogawa. The last thing I want is to be kicked off the baseball team for talking back to my teacher. That would be a disaster. The anger suddenly whooshes out of my body, and my arms go limp. I nod and slump down into my seat.

"I'm sorry, sir," I say, just loud enough for him to hear. I keep my head down for the rest of the class.

• • •

To distract myself, I replay my last game with the Bobcats in my head. I remember how my teammate Sean stole home base, how Jamal hit a triple, how I jumped into the air to snag a fly ball. But then I remember how sad I felt when it was over, knowing that my team would dissolve at least until the following spring, how I'd be practicing shadow swings in my backyard while the other guys moved on to football and wrestling and basketball. I think of how at this school, baseball is a full-time, year-round thing, and this makes me so happy that I almost forget about Mr. Tanaka.

10

That evening, when I get home, everything seems calm. Oji-chan and Momoko are at the kitchen table doing origami. Squares of brightly colored paper folded into animals and flowers are scattered across the table.

I point to a purple rabbit. "Did you make this?" I sign.

Momoko nods. She makes bunny ears with her hands.

"Good!" I make a fist, hold it to my nose, and pull.

She carefully picks it up and hands it to me.

"A present?"

She nods again, and signs, "For Misa."

So, I'm supposed to give this to her at school? Yeah, right. But if I refuse, Momoko will never stop nagging, so I nod and pretend that I'll do as I said.

● ● ●

At lunch the next day Junji brings a pack of beef jerky.

"Man, how can you survive on that?" I ask him. I lift the lid of my bento—sausages, a hard-boiled egg, cherry tomatoes, edamame, and rice balls. "Here, have a couple of these," I say, lifting a rice ball with my chopsticks. He holds out his hand and I drop it into his palm.

"Thanks."

Shintaro's bento is jam-packed, but of course he doesn't offer to share with Junji. He just shovels the food into his mouth, oblivious to our starving teammate.

I feel kind of sorry for him. I wonder if he wishes he had a mother like mine, one who gets up early every day and makes a big breakfast and lunch. His mom seems kind of lazy. But maybe I shouldn't think badly of his family. I mean, Oji-chan is losing his mind. So my family isn't perfect, I guess.

"I can't believe my grandfather showed up at practice yesterday," I say.

Junji shrugs, his mouth stuffed full of rice. After he swallows he says, "My grandmother is always wandering around, too. Sometimes we have to call the volunteer fire department to help us find her. Once, the whole neighborhood was out looking half the night."

"Where did she go?"

"Someone found her sitting in a rice paddy. She didn't even know where she was," Junji says.

"I'm still hungry," Shintaro suddenly announces. His lunch box looks as if he licked it clean. He slaps his belly and looks slowly around the room. He hones in on Misa. I feel a twinge of guilt at not having given her the origami bunny that my sister made for her, as if that tiny paper creature might be a good substitute for an actual friend.

Shintaro stands up and creeps over to her desk where Misa's eating alone, as usual. He reaches over her shoulder and snatches her sandwich. He stuffs most of it into his mouth.

My jaw drops. I can't believe he just stole her lunch.

Worse, he starts gagging dramatically. He leans over the wastebasket and spits out a glob of chewed bread. "Ugh. What was that? Grape jelly and peanut butter?"

Peanut butter and jelly. My old buddy Jamal's favorite sandwich. Misa's American mom must have introduced her to it.

There's still a hard-boiled egg and a cherry tomato in my bento box. I start to get up out of my chair to give them to her, but before I know it, she's gathered up her stuff and left the room. She doesn't come back for the rest of the day.

11

That afternoon during practice, Coach has us gather around for a lesson in signs.

Left hand tapping at the left shoulder, then right shoulder, then right forearm means "swing at anything." Right hand touching cap, then chest, then left shoulder means "bunt if it's a strike." Left hand on cap, chest, right shoulder means "bunt at anything—suicide squeeze."

"The guys at non-academic schools aren't smart enough to remember these," Junji whispers to me. "We have an advantage."

I feel sweat breaking out in my armpits, at the small of my back. I'm not sure that I'm smart enough either. But if I want to play for this team, I've got to get them down.

"Okay, guys. We're going to scrimmage now," Coach says. He breaks us up into two teams.

Junji and I are on the same side. We get Kikawa for pitcher. Lucky us! Kikawa, who is also team captain, is going to be our coach for the scrimmage. He's been around for a couple of years, so he's already memorized the signs.

Coach and the managers, Tomomi and Maki, settle in to canvas-backed director's chairs on the sidelines. Coach folds his arms and his face goes blank. The girls are holding clipboards. They'll be keeping track of every move we make.

Kikawa and the other side's pitcher, Onishi, a third-year southpaw, do *janken*—rock, paper, scissors—to decide who goes first. Kikawa's scissors lose to Onishi's rock. We're out in the field.

With Kikawa on the mound, there's not a lot happening in the outfield. I watch as he disposes of the first three batters with only ten tosses of the ball. After the third out, we hustle off the field and my team is up at bat.

In the third inning I finally get my turn. The first pitch is a little low. The second one comes straight down the middle, and I swing. The ball shoots past the short stop, into an unoccupied patch in left field. I make it to second base.

My teammates cheer and slap their hands

together. I feel that buzz I get every time I hear applause. I look over at Coach. He's still wearing his poker face, his arms are still folded, but they seem looser somehow.

Next up is Junji.

I look over at Kikawa. He pinches the bill of his cap, pats his chest, then his left shoulder—signal for a bunt.

Junji nods. He steps forward in the batter's box, angles his bat, and puts his face close to it, like he's smelling it.

I crab-walk off the base and crouch midway between second and third. I'm ready to make my move, but then Onishi pivots and pulls back his arm. He's going to try to throw me out, but I'm fast, quick as lightning, and I dive for second, scraping the heel of my hand on the gravel as I reach for the bag. My fingertips touch the base a split second before the ball arrives.

"Almost got you, America," Shintaro mutters. He's manning second in this game, though I'm sure he'd rather pitch.

"Almost doesn't count," I shoot back under my breath. I stand up and brush the dirt off my pants.

The next pitch is a little high. Junji doesn't bite. I stay put, but then Onishi lobs a strike and Junji lays it softly in the dirt a few feet in front of home plate.

I'm off. I make it safely to third as Onishi rushes in to scoop up the ball and fire it to first. It's an easy play, but the first baseman fumbles the ball. Junji touches first and flies on toward second.

The third base coach starts windmilling his arms. "Keep going! Keep going!"

I run as fast as I can, legs churning, heart thumping, my eyes fixed on home plate. When my foot comes down square in the middle, I hear shouts and chanting: "Sa-to-shi! Sa-to-shi!" Suddenly I feel like I could run all the way home and back again, all the way up Mt. Bizan, all the way to Osaka! I slap palms with my teammates, then look over to the sidelines. Tomomi is biting her lip and looking toward first base, maybe feeling sorry for the kid who committed an error. Maki is beaming at me. And Coach? He isn't smiling, but he nods his head slightly. I think I might have impressed him.

I can tell that my hand is bleeding, but I don't look at it. Adrenaline is zinging through my veins.

Tomomi comes over with the first aid kit and cleans my wound.

I keep my eyes on her face.

"Nice hit," she says.

"Thanks." The antiseptic stings a little, but I don't flinch.

When she's through, I take a swig from my thermos and watch the rest of the inning.

The other side gets a couple of hits next time around, but doesn't score. By the time I'm up at bat again, our guys are ahead 3-0. We've got a runner on first, and no outs.

I go through a few practice swings before stepping into the box. This time, I think, I'm going to hit it over the fence. But then I look over at Kikawa. He touches his cap, his chest, his left shoulder. Bunt? No way! We're winning and everyone has seen how I can hit. I shake my head almost imperceptibly.

Kikawa frowns and nods. He repeats the gestures.

Okay, I get it. This isn't a high stakes tournament game, it's just friendly play among teammates. Coach is probably checking to see if we've remembered the signs. So even though bunting at this point makes no sense, I square up in the batter's box and lower my bat.

The pitch comes in a little high, but I kiss it with the bat. It pops up... and plops down, right into the catcher's mitt. I'm out, and the runner is still on first. *Chikusho!* I could have hit that ball. I could have gotten a home run. I kick up a cloud of dirt, and then slouch back toward the dug-out, avoiding my teammates' eyes.

Our side wins anyway.

At the end of practice, as I'm shoving my gear

back into my bag, Coach taps me on the shoulder.

"That was some nice batting," he says.

"Thank you." I duck my head, trying to be modest. I don't mean to brag, but I'm sort of used to hearing this kind of praise. I heard it all the time from Coach Harris and my teammates in Atlanta, but I'm glad that Coach Ogawa recognizes my ability.

"But you need to work on your bunting," he adds.

My bunting? In the States, no one cares about the bunt. There were a few guys on my team who were masters at laying the ball in the dirt—not me—but it wasn't a necessary skill. It was far better to be able to blast the ball out of the park, which is something I can do.

I'm not about to say all that to the coach, however. Instead, I look up at him and say, "Yes, sir. I'll do my best."

He nods his head, just slightly.

12

When I get home, the lights are blazing in Oji-chan's quarters. I slide open his door and peer inside. *"Tadaima!"*

"Oh, hey, Satoshi," Oji-chan calls from the other room. "We're in here."

I find him and Momoko sitting around the low table, which is littered with tangerine peels and crayons. They're coloring pictures of princesses and unicorns. Geez, couldn't Okaasan have gotten my grandfather something more manly? A dinosaur coloring book? Baseball?

The TV's on, broadcasting the local news. Right now, there's a story about a live seal that turned up in the Yoshino River. No one knows where it came from. There are no seals missing from the zoo, and it doesn't seem likely that it would have swum all the way from Hokkaido.

"Hey, there's a friend for Nana-chan," I joke, nodding toward the TV screen.

"So there is," Oji-chan says, though he doesn't seem to be kidding. He glances over to the corner by the electrical outlet, where Nana-chan is hooked up to her recharging pacifier.

Momoko looks up from her coloring book and notices me. A smile breaks out on her face. "Misa!" she signs. "Coming to dinner!"

Oh, no. "When?" I ask.

"Saturday!"

• • •

The next morning at school Misa doesn't look at me when I walk past her desk. She probably wants to keep the fact that we know each other a secret. To tell the truth, I'm a little bit relieved. I'd rather not have the whole school know that our mothers are becoming friends and that she's coming over to my house for dinner. I'd rather not have to explain to Junji or my other teammates. It's none of their business after all.

I spend most of the day staring at the back of Misa's head willing her to keep quiet, and then it's time for baseball practice.

After we've changed into our uniforms and gathered on the field, Coach directs us into the clubhouse. This is where we lift weights and have meetings. "Okay, guys. Pop quiz," he says. He tells us to scatter, so that we can't look at anyone else's answers, and hands out papers.

The quiz is on the signs that we learned the day before. As soon as I pick up my pencil, sweat breaks out along my hairline. I take a deep breath and try to focus. Okay, I know the answer to the first one. If Coach touches his left ear, the previous sequence is negated. I'm pretty confident of the next answer, too, and the one after that. I finish the test, and then check my answers once again. When I finally look up, I see that I'm the last guy in the room.

Coach nods when I turn in my paper. "Okay, go run some laps," he says.

We go through our usual drills. We run across the field with tires yoked to our shoulders for strength training. We hit at wiffle balls with shovels. And then there's a short scrimmage. At the end of the session, I go up to Coach and tell him that I want to put in a little extra batting practice.

"I want to work on my bunting."

"Great!"

Most of the guys get on their bikes and go home, but I spend the next hour following Coach's every command: "Keep the bat at the top of the strike zone! Don't ever go higher!" "Use your knees!" "Pivot your back foot!" "No jabbing!"

I keep at it until Coach sends me home. I do this every day for the rest of the week, until I'm the best bunter on the team.

13

On Friday, when I leave for school, the sky is overcast. Rain starts falling at the start of first period and doesn't let up all day. Instead of practice on the field, Coach tells us to stay inside and lift weights.

The weather clears by morning, so our game with the Tokushima Hawks is on, as planned, but we have to gather at six a.m. to prepare the ground.

"Grab some buckets and rags," Kikawa says. "We need to sop up those puddles."

I pick up an aluminum pail and an old towel and find myself a puddle. I crouch down, dip the towel in the muddy water, and wring it out over the pail. I can't imagine Coach Harris ever making us do something so pointless. He'd want us to save our energy for the game. At my school in Atlanta, there was someone else who watered the grass and smoothed the dirt. Someone who got paid for doing it.

I soak up some more water with the towel, wring it out again. It's tedious, but it doesn't require any thinking.

The game time has been delayed for a couple of hours to give us a chance to get our diamond ready. After we've been crouching long enough to cramp our legs, and our buckets are full, we are sent to fill a wheelbarrow with fresh dirt and fill in the holes. After that, the raking.

Today I'm not even on the roster. Me and the rest of the first years will just be watching. The ninth graders are the only ones who get to play.

When the Hawks' bus finally pulls up, my teammates seem to shrink a little. I suddenly feel smaller, too. Their guys swagger, while the rest of us are now scuttling around like beetles. I can't help thinking that the Hawks are the tougher team. We may have brains, but our school's baseball team has never beaten theirs in a tournament.

I sit down in a folding chair on the sidelines with the rest of my first- and second-year teammates. Spectators usually don't show up for practice games in Japan, but some parents come to watch and help out. My dad is in Tokyo until tonight, but my mother dropped off Oji-chan before she set out on an errand. He's seated, leaning forward, ready for action. When I catch his eye, he winks at me. I give him a small salute.

Some other kids' mothers surround him in folding chairs, and a big, hulking guy stands behind home base. With his fingers hooked through the chain link fence, he looks like a tiger trying to get out of his cage. I realize that it's Shintaro's dad.

Shintaro, two seats down from me, is frowning. His shoulders are stiff. I watch for a while to see if he acknowledges his father. His eyes dart to the side from time to time, as if checking to see if his dad is still there, but he never turns his head.

Before the start of the game, both teams rush out to the center of the field, line up, and bow to each other. I notice that the Hawks' bowing is short and shallow. I guess their coach isn't big on humility. But as the game gets underway, I see that they have no reason to be so cocky.

Our teams are pretty evenly matched. Not a lot happens in the first several innings, which makes the game kind of boring. The chair gets harder and harder under my butt. Next to me,

Junji's knee jerks up and down. Yuji, the first-year catcher, seems lost in some daydream. By the seventh inning, there are still no runs. If only someone would get on base!

And then Shima, our number four batter, gets a nice line drive into right field. The ball nearly grazes the foul line, but it's in play. As the outfielders scramble after it, Shima rounds first base and goes on to second. He's cutting it close.

"Slide!" the third base coach calls out.

The rest of us jump up to cheer him on.

"Go, Shima!" I shout, my feet pounding the ground as if I were running with him.

Shima goes into a skid, but somehow, he gets tangled up with the second baseman. Limbs are going every which way. A cloud of dust rises. Shima goes down in a heap, with his leg at a weird angle. I'm not sure, but I think I hear a crack. Shima starts to howl.

Kikawa calls a time out, and the coaches and managers rush onto the field with a first aid kit. From the sidelines, I can't really see what's going on. All I can hear is Shima roaring like a lion, and then Coach saying the words "ambulance" and "don't move him."

I imagine a pool of blood and start to feel a little sick to my stomach.

A few minutes later, Kikawa runs over to tell us that the game is over. Final score 0-0. It's only a practice game, anyhow. It doesn't really matter if we finish the game or not. It won't go down in the record books. Still, I notice that Shintaro's dad shakes his head in disgust and slinks away. As soon as he's gone, Shintaro loosens up.

"Our team could totally beat theirs," Shintaro says in a loud voice.

It's true. We didn't lose. These guys are legendary, but they couldn't even score. That means that we have a chance to win in the summer tournament. I guess we should feel happy that our team wasn't bitterly defeated, that our guys held their own, but all I can think about is the commotion on the field.

Out of the corner of my eye, I see Oji-chan getting up from his chair. Suddenly, he's right behind me, whispering in my ear. "That kid is out of the game now," he says. "You've got a chance to take his spot."

14

When I get home from baseball, all grimy and sweaty, I find a strange blue car parked in front of our house. Ugh. I'd completely forgotten. We have company.

Maybe I can sneak into my room without being noticed. I open up the front door as quietly as possible.

"Here he is!" Okaasan's voice rings out in English. "Come on in here and say 'hello' to our guests."

I take a deep breath and pause at the threshold of the living room. There she is, Misa, the girl I'm not supposed to talk to, sitting at a low table, folding paper with my sister. Momoko is holding up a pink giraffe, a big smile on her face.

"Hi, Misa," I say. "Hi, Mr. and Mrs. Watanabe."

Her parents are sitting on the sofa with glasses

of wine. Her mom is wearing a red dress and dangly earrings, and her dad is wearing a polo shirt and khakis. Everyone looks nice and clean.

"Uh, I guess I'd better take a shower."

While the water sprays over me, I try to think of things to say to Misa. Like, "Sorry, Shintaro was such a jerk the other day." And, "Congrats on getting such a high score on that last test."

By the time I come back, dinner's on the table. My dad is passing around plates of spaghetti with tomato sauce. Momoko is sitting next to Misa, trying to teach her some signs. She twirls her three middle fingers—the sign for "spaghetti." Looks like I won't have to entertain my classmate after all. They seem to be having a good time.

We're all speaking in English—all of us except Momoko, that is—so it's almost like being back in the States. I feel weirdly relieved.

Okaasan starts going on about how in Atlanta all of the streets seem to be named after peaches. "I was always getting confused!" she says.

Misa's mom laughs. "Well, at least the streets have names. Here, I can never find my way because they don't have any names at all."

Misa rolls her eyes. "Just use the map app on

your smart phone." Her English is perfect.

After dinner, Okaasan hauls out some English board games—Monopoly, Life, and Scrabble.

I've got a better idea. "Wanna play Wii baseball?" I ask Misa.

"Oka-a-a-y. But what about Momoko? Won't she feel left out?"

"She can play, too. She's good at it. You'll see."

The adults hang out at the table, talking and drinking coffee, while we kids go into the living room. After a while, Oji-chan pops in to say "hello." He comes to cheer us on.

"Do you want to play, too?" I ask him after a couple of innings.

"No, I think I'd better go check on Nana-chan." He winks. I can't tell for sure if he's kidding or not. Maybe he just wants to get back to some peace and quiet.

"Okay. Next time, then."

He shuffles off to his quarters.

"Who's Nana-chan?" Misa asks after he's out of hearing.

"Ummm his pet seal robot…"

Misa raises her eyebrows.

"I'll introduce you to her next time." Next time?

Ugh. Why did I say that? It's not like I'm planning to make her my best friend. People will talk. It would be bad for both of us. But what can I say? I can feel myself blushing.

Just then, Momoko gets a home run. She yelps and holds her palms up for a high-five. I slap my hands against hers, and Misa gives her a hug. Phew. The awkward moment is over.

15

In another week, Coach will be announcing the names of the sixteen players who will be playing in the summer tournament. Sunday's practice is intense, and everyone seems to be trying harder than before. It's as if all of us are vying for Shima's spot. During our scrimmage, while stuck out in right field, Kenta, another first-year student, goes racing after a ball that's clearly foul. Junji is especially focused at the plate and hits a double. And me, I show everyone just how well I can bunt.

My second time at bat, I'm up against Shintaro. He's been throwing a little high and outside for most of the afternoon, but his first pitch almost grazes my knees. I jump back to avoid getting hit.

"Ball one," calls out the kid who's serving as umpire.

The second pitch is outside. I swing and miss.

And then I square up, determined to hit the third. No one's thrown out the bunt sign. This time I want to bash it to the far end of the field.

Shintaro scowls at me. I see his lips move, but I can't tell what he's saying. He reaches down, picks up some chalk and rubs it between his fingers. And then he goes into his wind-up and fires.

I can see the ball coming, can almost feel the blast of pain before it hits my thigh. The impact makes me cry out. "Arggh!" I drop my bat and fall to the ground, gripping my leg.

Coach rushes over. "Are you okay?"

On the mound, Shintaro doffs his cap and bows in apology. *"Sumimasen."* Okay, so maybe it was accidental, but I doubt it. Shintaro would be happy to see me out of the game. He wants that vacant spot just as much as I do.

Tomomi brings a can of cold spray and Coach blasts my thigh. It'll be black and blue tomorrow, for sure.

"Want me to put in a runner for you?" Coach asks.

No way. This is no time to look like a wimp. I grit my teeth. "It's okay. I'll run." And then I get up, brush myself off, and jog over to first base.

At the end of practice, when our gear is stowed and the field is raked smooth, Coach gathers us around.

"Starting tomorrow," he says, "I expect to see you out here at six thirty. We'll be having morning practice in addition to afternoon sessions until the tournament."

No one groans, no one protests. Instead, we all stand with our backs straight and say, *"Hai!"*

16

Monday, during Home Room, Mr. Tanaka tells us that he's made a new seating chart. I'm now in the front row, off to the right. It feels like a punishment. Misa is in the same row, but four sets behind me. And now that I'm in the first row, with no one to hide behind, Mr. Tanaka can tell whenever I'm not paying attention.

When it's time for English class, he shows up with Jerry. This time, Jerry is wearing black Crocs as slippers and he's carrying a guitar in one hand. In the other, he holds a sheaf of papers.

"Good-o moaning-goo!" Mr. Tanaka says.

"Good morning," we all reply.

"Today, we are happy to have Mr. Jerry here to teach us a famous American song," Mr. Tanaka says in a jovial voice. He surrenders his class to Jerry, and sits behind his desk.

"Hi, everybody." Jerry starts passing out sheets of paper.

When I get mine, I see that he's given us the lyrics to "This Land is Your Land," along with an illustrated map, designating places such as "the Redwood Forest" and "the New York island."

He sings it once, inviting us to just listen. His voice is surprisingly good. He may not be Justin Bieber, but he can definitely carry a tune. Out of the corner of my eye, I see my classmates bobbing their heads. Even Mr. Tanaka nods along, although he doesn't open his mouth.

"Okay, this time everybody sing it with me!" Jerry says. "One, two, three..." He starts strumming again.

I can hear Shintaro's voice, loud and off-key. He's mocking the song, but at least he's singing. Underneath, Misa's pure tones seep through. She has a great voice.

We're just getting into it, ready for a third round, when Mr. Tanaka stands up and claps loudly. "Thank you so much, Mr. Jerry. Now you can sit down over there. Our regular class will begin."

Jerry looks surprised, but he nods sheepishly and sits down, the guitar resting on his lap.

Mr. Tanaka writes a list of English idioms on the black board, the chalk squeaking every third or fourth word.

"It's raining cats and dogs."

"These are the dog days of summer."

"It's a dog eat dog world."

I know some of them. Others I'm sure I can get away without using for the rest of my life, but Mr. Tanaka tells us we never know when one of these expressions might turn up on an important test. I write a few in my notebook while trying not to yawn. Mr. Tanaka comes close to my desk and stands there for a moment. It feels like a threat. Finally, he saunters away toward the back of the classroom.

I glance over at Jerry. His chin is on his chest. It looks like he's nodded off.

I'm suddenly drained of energy, too tired to care about cats and dogs and the rain coming down. I've been up since five a.m. because we had our first morning practice session today. I put my head down—just for a minute—and fall asleep.

I'm dreaming that I'm tucked into my futon. Everything is warm and soft. My body is totally relaxed. And then... thwack!

My head jerks up. "Wh-what?" I wipe the drool off my chin.

Mr. Tanaka is standing in front of my desk again, this time with a rolled-up notebook in his hand.

I rub the back of my head where he hit me.

"Did you have a nice nap?" he asks in a syrupy voice.

Didn't he see us running with tires at seven this morning? Doesn't he know that we'll have practice again this afternoon until well after dark? Then after that, we'll go home and study?

I apologize, just to get Mr. Tanaka away from me.

He studies me for a long moment, then, apparently satisfied that I've been humiliated enough, goes back to the front of the class.

I catch Jerry's eye. The commotion has obviously woken him up, too. Now he looks worried, and a little guilty. Maybe he thinks that Mr. Tanaka is angry that he fell asleep during his mind-numbing English lesson and is taking it out on me. It's not as if he can wallop the visiting teacher, after all.

After class, he comes up to me. "Are you okay?" he asks in a low voice.

"I'm fine," I say, with a glance at Mr. Tanaka. "It was nothing. My dad used to get smacked in the forehead with a wooden ruler for being late to class when he was a kid. That must have hurt more."

Jerry's jaw drops. I know what it's like in America. Teachers aren't even allowed to pat a kid on the back. But here, things are different. When Oji-chan played baseball, his coach punished players with a swing of the bat against their rear ends. Of course, that's against the rules these days, but a lot of coaches and teachers still slap kids around, and get away with it.

"Seriously," I assure Jerry. "I'm fine."

At lunchtime, Misa disappears. I think of how Shintaro swiped her sandwich the other day. Maybe she's hiding from him. I hope she's not eating all alone in a corner somewhere.

• • •

That afternoon when I get home, I find Misa coloring with Oji-chan and Momoko.

"How's your head?" she asks me.

I'm too surprised to answer her question. "What are you doing here?" Does she think we're buddies now, just because she came over for dinner one time?

Her face falls. "Your mom invited me to hang out with Momoko. Sort of like a babysitter."

"Oh." I guess that's a good idea, especially since Momoko doesn't have any friends around here. All of the other kids in the neighborhood go to a different school. Nobody plays outside. If they're not at school, they're cramming with tutors somewhere.

Misa holds out a blue crayon. "Do you want to color with us?"

"Uh, no thanks."

She shrugs and goes back to filling in the lines of a unicorn.

Since she's here anyway, I can talk to her, I guess. I still feel bad about not sticking up for her when Shintaro ruined her lunch. "I'm sorry about what Shintaro did the other day," I blurt out.

She continues coloring. "Don't worry about it. I'm used to it."

"So where have you been eating lunch?" *Please don't say the toilet stall.*

She puts down her crayon and looks up. There's a sparkle in her eyes. "I go to English lunch with Mr. Jerry."

"English lunch?" First time I've ever heard about that.

"It's only for special people, but I guess I can tell you. It's up on the third floor in the room next to where we have Art." She switches out the blue crayon for a red one and goes back to shading. "You should come."

"Hmmm." If it's so secret that even Shintaro and Junji don't know about it, I guess I can get away with joining once or twice. It would be fun to be able to speak English once in a while so I don't forget the words that I know. "Thanks," I say. "Maybe I will."

• • •

Later, I check my email. There's a message from Rico. The subject line reads "Pool party!" I click open a photo of Rico, floating in an inflated ring, sunglasses pushed on top of his head.

Jamal has sent me, and about a million of his friends, a joke. It has something to do with a duck walking into a bar. I read it twice, but I still don't get it.

17

On the first day of June, we get to ditch the jackets and ties and wear short sleeves. It's the best time of year in Japan—warm, a little breezy, right before the beginning of the rainy season. A month-and-a-half before the start of the summer tournament.

Today Coach will make his big announcement. We'll find out who is going to be out on the field for the tournament. Sixteen players will be chosen. The rest of us will be batboys and water bearers during practice. The guys who don't get picked will be cheering from the stands.

I can hardly choke down my lunch. I can't concentrate during English or science or math. During Japanese class, I look over at Junji. His fuzzy head is nested in his arms. From across the room, I can hear him snoring gently but Miss

Hashimoto doesn't try to wake him up. She must be a baseball fan.

I turn all the way around in my seat to glance at Misa, but she's writing and doesn't meet my eyes.

Finally, the last bell chimes. I pick up my books, then go over and nudge Junji.

"It's time," I say.

We go up to second floor together, to Coach Ogawa's home room. We sit at the desks in our crisp white shirts and plaid pants, all serious, like prisoners awaiting a sentence.

Some of these guys already know that they'll be on the team. Most of the guys who played in the spring tournament will be playing in summer. But a few spots are up for grabs. I know that I'm good enough to be on the team. I have to be on the team. No one wants to win as badly as I do. I have to win for Oji-chan.

Coach Ogawa steps up to the front of the classroom. He's wearing a tie with a baseball motif and his cheeks look freshly shaven. There are bags under his eyes, though, and I wonder if he stayed up all night fretting over the sixteen. He wants to win just as much as anybody.

He clears his throat. "Good afternoon."

We respond in sync. "Good afternoon, Coach!"

"As you know, the summer tournament begins next month. You've all played your hearts out for this moment, and I've been moved by your efforts. If it were up to me, you'd all be on the roster, taking your turns at bat." He pauses and looks at every one of us. When his eyes meet mine, he holds his gaze steady. "But even if I don't call your name today, you should know that you are still a valuable member of this team. We need your support during practice, and we need you to keep up the spirits of the players on the field. Your job is very important."

I feel my stomach sink.

Hata, over there by the wall, will probably be on the team. He plays third base, and he can whack the ball if he wants to, if he's in the zone. His father's been helping out a lot at weekend practices. I've heard that he sometimes invites Coach Ogawa out for yakitori and beer after Saturday's practice sessions. "To butter up." There's another idiom. Hata's dad "buttered up" the coach.

And Kikawa, there at the back of the room, was personally recruited by Coach Ogawa. Three or four different coaches had been after him. They went all the way out to the elementary school in a little fishing village where he was a student to see him pitch. Kikawa's parents had convinced him to go with Ogawa and Tokushima Whirlpool Junior High. And now Coach Ogawa is responsible for him. I'm sure he'll start.

But Shima broke his leg, and a couple other players haven't had their heads in the game lately. They're not as good as some of us second-year players. There's at least one opening. Maybe two or three.

The managers bring in a stack of brand-new jerseys and set them on the podium.

Coach rattles off a little more about team spirit and sacrifice and then he reads the first name.

"Hai!" The third-year first baseman stands up, his back straight as a soldier's, and walks to the front of the room. He bows first to the rest of the team, then to Coach Ogawa. Then he holds out both hands and accepts the new uniform as if it were a diploma or an award, and bows again.

"I will fight hard for everyone!" he says. His expression is stoic, blank, but I can imagine the wild joy leaping inside of him.

Coach looks down at his list.

Pick me! Pick me! I think.

"Kikawa Ryohei," he calls out.

Of course. We can't do anything without him.

Kikawa pushes back his chair and goes to the front of the room.

I remember the moment that Coach Harris in Atlanta read my name, and how I felt as if I could hurl a ball all the way to the moon. I hadn't thought I had a chance. After all, I was an outsider, a foreigner, some stranger from Japan. I wasn't part of the system. I hadn't grown up going to the same schools and playing on the same Little League team as everyone else. My dad didn't go out drinking with the coach. But in America, none of that mattered.

A bunch of boys had shown up for the first practice sessions—white kids, African-Americans, and guys who spoke to each other in Spanish. I totally blended in until I picked up a bat. When I blasted the ball, I heard a buzz go up around me. "Wow!" Someone said. "This kid is magic!"

Coach calls out another name. His voice pulls me back to Japan, back into this room.

"Okada Soichiro."

The third-year short stop goes up and gets his uniform.

Coach goes down the list until there's only one spot left. Not a single first or second-year student has been named to the team so far. I feel sweat breaking out along my hairline and under my arms. My hands grip my knees under the desk and my teeth are clenched. Out of the corner of my eye, I see Junji straining forward.

And then, finally, "Matsumoto Satoshi."

"Yes!"

I feel like bumping fists or slapping hands with someone, but when I look around me, there is no joy. A few of the ninth graders who didn't make the team are giving me the evil eye. Junji is sitting there with his shoulders slumped, looking down. Shintaro's name wasn't called either. He's good enough to make the team, I know, but he doesn't seem to be angry at me for taking his place. Instead, he's looking out the window, biting his thumbnail. If anything, he looks worried. I wonder if his dad will cuss him out because he wasn't selected.

The room is silent. I'm suddenly embarrassed for shouting. *"Sumimasen,"* I mumble. *I'm sorry.*

I stand and walk up to Coach Ogawa. He hands me the uniform that I will wear for tournament play, and then I put on my super-serious face and bow to him and my teammates. "I will do my best to help this team get to the championship round," I say.

Then I sit back down.

Coach explains that from now until the tournament, only the chosen players will be participating in practices. He has a list of tasks for everyone else, which he turns over to Kikawa, our team captain.

"Okay, now, get out there on the field."

The ceremony is over. The guys shuffle out of the room. I expect Junji to congratulate me, or at least walk to the clubhouse with me, but he hangs back with Shintaro. He doesn't say a thing.

18

The big freeze continues throughout afternoon practice and on into the next day. At lunchtime, Junji pushes his desk next to Shintaro's. I move my desk over by theirs, but they ignore me. Shintaro has a lacquer box stuffed with rice balls, fish, and boiled vegetables. He doesn't offer anything to Junji, who's dining on a bag of rolls. He probably bought them at the convenience store on the way to school. I eat my bento without saying a word.

Junji and Shintaro are laughing about something, and I'm not in on the joke. I don't know why they're being such jerks. Maybe they think I'm getting special treatment from the coach because my grandfather founded the school. Or maybe they think it's because I went to America. What they don't understand is that if we don't win, there will be no more baseball. I can help us win. I know I can.

I glance over at Misa's empty desk. Might as well go check out English lunch.

"Excuse me," I mutter.

I pack up my half-eaten lunch and move my desk away from theirs. Other students look up at the screech of dragging furniture.

Junji and Shintaro continue ignoring me at first. But then they go silent and I feel their eyes on my back as I walk out the door.

Third floor, next to the Art room, she said. I climb the stairs and find the room. The door's closed. With my ear against the wood, I can make out voices. Laughter. English. I knock lightly. Wait.

The voices stop. I hear footsteps, then the door slides open wide enough for one eye to peer through.

"Oh, it's you!" Misa says. She slides the door open wider.

"Hey." I try to sound all casual, even though my heart is knocking around my rib cage. If I held out my hands, they'd probably be shaking.

"Hi." She slides the door open wider.

"Hey, there, Satoshi," Jerry says. He's sitting at a table with a pile of sandwiches. "Come on in. You know Misa already, right? This is Masaki and Shina."

Next to him is a boy with a weight problem from another class, and a girl with an eye patch—bully magnets all. "English Lunch" is clearly code name for "losers."

I nod at everyone, drop into an empty chair, and gobble the rest of my bento's contents in silence.

The others seem super self-conscious at first, sliding their eyes at me, as if afraid I'll attack. When they figure out that I'm not there to hurt them, they seem to forget about me. Pretty soon they start talking again. "Hey, can we play Trivial Pursuit again next week?" Shina asks. "That was really fun."

"Yes," Masaki adds. "I like that game. I've been studying so that I can win next time."

Wow. They all speak English really well. And Trivial Pursuit? I played that at Jamal's house, back in Atlanta. It *was* fun.

"Sure," Jerry says. He turns to me. "Do you want to play, too?"

"Uh, okay."

At the first bell, Misa and I walk back into the classroom together.

"Are your friends going to give you a hard time for being seen with me?" she asks under her breath.

Do you want to play, too?

They're looking our way now. Shintaro nudges Junji and says something. They break into laughter. Morons.

I shrug. "They're already giving me a hard time because I'm going to be playing in the summer tournament and they're not."

Her eyes go big. "Congratulations!"

"Thanks."

19

When I go up to the Art room for the secret losers' lunch the next day, the Trivial Pursuit game board is already set up.

"What color do you want to be?" Misa asks, waving a pie-shaped piece.

"Green," I say.

In between eating our lunches, we take turns rolling the dice and trying to answer questions.

When my turn comes around, I land on an orange space.

Shina picks up a card. "Orange is 'Sports and Leisure.' Okay, here goes. 'What country did Babe Ruth visit in 1934?'"

Easy. I grin. "Japan!"

"Huh," Misa says, handing over a tiny orange plastic wedge. "I didn't know that."

I pass the dice to Masaki, who makes a big

production of blowing on it before he tosses it across the table. Where does he think we are, Las Vegas?

"Your turn to read, Satoshi," Jerry says.

I see that he's landed on a blue space—the geography category. "'What three European countries begin with the letter 'A'?'"

He presses against the side of his nose with his index finger before answering, "Andorra, Albania, and Austria."

"Whoa. I'm impressed." Now we're tied. Game on.

We only make it halfway through the game by the end of lunch period, so we all promise to come back tomorrow. For the rest of the day, I do my best to ignore Junji and Shintaro, who are in turn ignoring me. During practice, Shintaro deliberately bumps into me with the rake and his elbows. He doesn't apologize. Junji doesn't talk to me at all.

On Wednesday, Misa doesn't show up at school. A couple of other kids are absent from our homeroom as well. So is Jerry. My stomach falls. No English lunch then, I guess.

Mr. Tanaka shows up wearing a white surgical mask over his nose and mouth.

"Good morning, everyone," he says in English.

His words are muffled, but we know the routine.

"Good morning, Mr. Tanaka!" the class responds automatically.

"How are you today?"

"I'm fine thank you, and you?"

"I'm fine, too."

But he doesn't look fine. His eyes are watery, and he coughs into the mask.

"You may have heard that the flu is going around," he says. "Today, there are twenty students absent from our school. I would advise you to wash your hands as often as possible, and to wear a mask."

There have been rumors about this new flu. The television and newspaper have reported school closings in other parts of Japan. In some places, drug stores have run out of masks, so people have been making them out of coffee filters and paper towels. Schools require sick students to stay away for ten days after getting a diagnosis.

Ten days is a long time to be away from baseball practice, especially with the summer tournament coming up. As soon as I can get to the store, I'm going to stock up on masks. This is no time to be sick.

Even though word got to Coach that I nearly fainted during lunch the other day, I managed to convince him that I was okay. I was just very tired. He's been watching me closely at practice, checking for signs of weakness. I've been running faster than usual, and hitting the ball twice as hard.

That afternoon, we're in the middle of fielding practice when one of the ladies who works in the school office comes out to the diamond. I see her talking with Coach, and then he calls me in from center field.

"Your mother called," he says, laying a hand on my shoulder. "Your grandfather has gone missing and she needs you to go help look for him."

Oh, no! An image of Oji-chan wandering around aimlessly in his pajamas and slippers jumps into my mind. What if he gets hit by a car or something? What if he's lost and can't even remember his own name? I glance out at the guys in the field. They're waiting for the next fungo, and here I am, holding them up. I feel a jolt of impatience. Why couldn't Okaasan have kept a better eye on him? And why did Oji-chan have to choose this of all possible moments to go walking around? Okay, okay, I know he doesn't get into trouble on purpose. If he'd been thinking straight, he'd know how important it is for me to be at practice. It's not his fault. He could be in danger. I've got to go.

● ● ●

The first-year players hanging out at the sidelines are all looking at me as I leave the diamond and untie my cleats. They look hostile, and hungry—eager to fill in as soon as I get kicked off the team.

I brush past Shima, hobbling around on crutches. He can't play, but he's here to lend moral support. He's still part of the team. I feel a little guilty when I see him, even though I'm not the one who broke his leg. "See you tomorrow," I say.

He nods.

I hit balls in my head all the way home. When I get there, Okaasan is standing in the yard in her apron, clutching her cell phone. She practically falls on me in relief.

"How long has he been missing?" I ask. I don't hear any public announcements blaring from a sound truck, so I know she hasn't called the volunteer fire department yet.

"A couple of hours, I guess," she says. "I brought him a cup of tea after lunch, and left him watching one of his videos. I hung out the laundry, and then someone called on the phone, and I got caught up and lost track of time."

"Well, he can't have gone far," I say.

She tells me that she's already checked the little roads near our house that meander through the rice paddies and sweet potato fields. She went to the neighborhood shrine and down to the riverbank where Oji-chan used to like to dig for smallneck clams at this time of year.

"I'll go see if he's anywhere near the cemetery," I say. Sometimes he goes to visit Obaachan's grave. Maybe he went there to chant a sutra, or to clean the tombstone.

Still in my baseball uniform, I set off on my bike for the Buddhist cemetery. I pass some boys with long nets, chasing after insects, and a man out for a cruise in his wheelchair. When I get to the cemetery, I don't see anyone. I check out my grandmother's grave. The leaves in the vases are dried and crumbling. No one has been here in a few days. My stomach drops.

Since I'm here anyway, I yank out the dried

twigs, fill a galvanized steel bucket with water from the spigot at the edge of the row of plots, and ladle some water over the stones. Now, where's Oji-chan?

I finally find him about a hundred meters away, standing in the driveway of a stranger's house, reading the nameplate on their gate. A chained dog is barking furiously at him. He has a bundle of leaves in his hands. It looks like he was on his way to the cemetery, and then got lost. I close my eyes for a second in relief.

"Oji-chan!" I shout, waving my arms furiously. "Wrong house!"

He turns slowly at the sound of my voice, but it takes a moment for recognition to fill his eyes. "Masahiro?" That's my dad's name.

I laugh. Good enough.

"Come on," I say, taking him by the arm. "Let's get you home."

20

"So, who are you boys going to be playing in the summer tournament?" Oji-chan asks me a couple days later when we're hanging out in his apartment.

"In game one, we'll be playing the Ikeda Wild Boars," I tell him. It's a school in the western part of Tokushima Prefecture.

He nods, then takes a sip of his tea. "They were national champs once, but they've got a weak team this year. You should be able to get past them easily."

In other good news, the Tokushima Hawks and the Naruto Ninjas, two baseball powerhouses, are pitted against each other. One major foe will be taken out in the first round. Furthermore, word has it that Seiko Junior High School's baseball team has been hit with the flu. Seiko is a private school, like ours, that draws players from all over the country. They usually make it to at least the quarterfinals, if not the semi-finals.

So far, our team is pretty healthy, although Junji doesn't show up for school the next day, and neither do Misa and Jerry.

At lunchtime, I eat by myself.

Just as I'm lifting the lid of my bento box, Shintaro comes up behind me. I guess he doesn't have anyone to talk to since Junji is out. He reaches over my shoulder and grabs a tomato out of my lunch box. Before I can say anything, he pops it into his mouth.

Up close, I notice that he's got a nasty bruise on his jaw.

"What happened to your face?"

"Walked into a door," he says quickly. "So where's your girlfriend?"

I angle my body away from his. "Shut up. She's not my girlfriend."

He reaches over my shoulder again, but this time I slam the lid on my bento box so he can't grab anything else. Part of me wants to punch him in the face, but that's a bad idea. I pick up my lunch and head for the lawn outside. I shouldn't let him chase me away, I know, but I don't feel like dealing with him today. And if we get into a fight, I could be suspended from the team.

I can't let Shintaro get to me. I need to be strong.

• • •

Misa finally shows up a week later for end-of-the-semester exams. I need to ace this exam. I brace myself for trick questions, but it's actually pretty easy—way easier than the Japanese test will be. This one is multiple choice, so I don't have to think too hard. I finish within thirty minutes then stretch out and look around.

Junji's mouth is moving silently as he reads over something on page two. I watch as he carefully marks an answer, then pauses over the next question. Shintaro, on the other hand, is staring out the window, his face crumpled into a frown. He probably didn't study. I remember how in elementary school he was always forgetting his homework. Well, that's his problem.

21

Momoko wants to know why Misa hasn't been around.

I hold my fist up to my forehead. "She was sick."

"I want her to come again," Momoko signs.

"Yeah, yeah. I'll tell her." At the moment, I have other things to think about. I've got to get my head in the game. With final exams out of the way, it's time to concentrate on the summer baseball tournament. Our team is strong, but we can use all the help we can get. On game day, I tuck a temple charm into my back pocket. My grandmother gave it to me a long time ago, when I was still in elementary school, for good fortune on the field. I had it with me during every important game in Atlanta, including the one where we became regional champs. As I mount my bike, I can smell incense coming from Oji-chan's quarters. I'm pretty sure he's chanting sutras for me, praying for our victory.

I'm pumped, and I pedal faster than usual to get on the bus bound for the stadium in Tokushima City. Now that the rain has lifted, the heat and humidity of summer have moved in. Even this early in the morning it feels as if a dragon is breathing down my back.

When I arrive at the school parking lot, I see that about half the guys have already gathered. A limo bus, hired for the day, is waiting, its engine idling.

"*Osu!*" I say in greeting.

My teammates tip their hats.

The school band is there, grappling with their instruments. Some volunteer parents are loading coolers of ice and cold drinks onto the bus. I see Junji across the tarmac and nod. He nods back, but he doesn't come over to talk. He's wearing his uniform, and his head is shaved in solidarity, but he and most of the rest of the first-year students will be in the cheering section today. They've got little megaphones and banners to hold up at key moments. Tomomi and Maki are holding long, colorful chains of origami cranes which will be hung in the dugout.

"Okay, guys, time to board," Coach Ogawa calls out. He motions toward the door of the bus.

I take a deep breath. My teammates are counting on me. Oji-chan is counting on me. The whole school. I need to get into the zone. I need to focus.

The stadium is about twenty minutes away, in a sports park at the base of Mt. Bizan. We stash our gear in the locker room, then dash out onto the field to warm up. Our game is the first of the day. Two more will follow.

I look up into the stands. There's Jerry, the American teacher. He gives me the thumbs-up. Some guy holding a camera with a long-lens is leaning over the fence—probably a reporter from the newspaper. I can see Otosan, who's back home for the weekend, and Oji-chan behind home plate, cooling themselves with paper fans. Okaasan is home with Momoko. There are a bunch of girls from school in the bleachers, all in their school uniform, white shirt and plaid skirt.

I pick out Shintaro's father. He's sitting just above our dugout, wearing sunglasses and working a toothpick in his mouth. He's with a couple of scary-looking guys with tattoos peeking out of their shirtsleeves.

"Matsumoto!"

"Hai! I turn at the sound of my name and run out into the outfield to shag some flies.

At exactly nine o'clock, a siren blares. We run onto the field, and line up. The national anthem is broadcast through loudspeakers. I feel a spark of pride as I watch the flag rising up the pole. In Atlanta, I never sang along to the "Star Spangled Banner," mostly because I didn't know the words. But here, I sing. *"Kimi ga yo..."* My voice blends with my teammates', with the voice of the crowd. For once, I feel like a link in the chain. And then it's time for the game to begin.

We're first up at bat.

Inoue hits the very first pitch, and makes it to first. A roar goes up in the stands. Tanaka, the second batter, lets the first strike go by, swings at an outside ball and misses, then winds up whiffing on the third. One out. And then Sagawa pounds a line drive into left field, and Tanaka makes it all the way to third.

Our brass band strikes up "Popeye, the Sailor Man." The cheering section begins to chant:

"Gan-ba-re! Gan-ba-re!"

Only minutes into the game, and already the opposing pitcher is looking flustered. He takes a moment to calm himself. I watch his shoulders hitch up as he takes a deep breath. Then he throws the ball across the plate, and Noda, our clean-up guy, pops it up into deep center field.

Tanaka waits for the catch, tags third, dashes for home. He slides into the base, beating the ball. And we're ahead, 1–0.

By the time my turn at bat comes up, two innings later, we've scored another run, and they're still at zero. I manage a two-base hit, and cross the finish line two batters later when Inoue is next up at the plate.

Ikeda changes pitchers in the fourth inning— never a good sign. And the game goes on like that. By the seventh inning, we've totally humiliated them. The game is called. Final score: 9–1.

The siren sounds again and both teams line up to bow. The guys from Ikeda are wiping at their eyes and noses. I'd almost forgotten about the crying. In America, if you cry after losing a game, you're a total wuss. In Japan, crying after a loss is almost required. If you don't show some emotion, everyone thinks you don't care.

Our school song is broadcast over the loudspeaker, and we all sing along. And then we bow to the friends and classmates and family members in the stands who have come to see us play. The captain from Ikeda's team presents Kikawa with the chain of origami cranes that had been made for their own team. These will be hung in our dugout at the next game, a week from today.

We hang around to watch the following match-up to get a sense of the competition. The Naruto Ninjas, one of the strongest teams in the prefecture, is paired up with the Tokushima Hawks. Naruto made it all the way to the semi-finals a couple of years ago, but today, they lose in the first round. Afterwards, of course, they start bawling like babies.

We take the bus back to school for a post-game debriefing.

"Let's go celebrate," Kikawa says, once the meeting is over and our gear is stowed. "Anyone up for some noodles?"

My stomach growls. "I am!"

A few more guys chime in, and we agree to bike over to an udon restaurant near school.

At three in the afternoon, the restaurant is nearly empty. We quickly fill up the booths. Our voices and laughter drown out the sound of the TV on the wall. A woman my mom's age in a white apron and kerchief brings us cups of green tea and then goes around with her pad, taking orders for noodles with seaweed, noodles with tempura, and noodles with fried tofu.

Right now, with a two-base hit behind me, a steaming bowl of noodles in front of me, and my teammates all around, I can't think of anyplace I'd rather be. If I were in Atlanta right now, I wouldn't even be playing baseball. The season is over. Everyone's on summer vacation, looking ahead to football. But here, we're on the brink of something big. If we win the next two games, we'll be in the semifinals. And then we're one game away from the championship.

After finishing his noodles, Junji comes up behind me and claps a hand on my shoulder. "Nice hit," he says.

"Thanks." I guess this is his way of apologizing for being a jerk. I'm ready to forgive him.

22

In the next game, I hit a home run and we win with a score of 7–2. Then we take on Seiko, and defeat them 5-4. Some of their players are still out with the flu, so it doesn't seem entirely fair, but we celebrate anyhow. Our next game, the semi-final, is against the Tokushima Hawks.

"There's no reason why we can't beat them," Coach Ogawa tells us after Friday's practice. "You guys put up a fine performance in that practice game this past spring. You proved that you're just as good as they are."

That was the game where Shima broke his leg, the game that determined my future.

We're all standing around the coach, our uniforms soaked with sweat. The screech of cicadas fills the air.

"They're just kids," Coach says. "They put their

uniform pants on one leg after another, just like you and me."

A few guys chuckle.

"Go home, eat your dinner, and get a good night's sleep. I'll see you here tomorrow at seven a.m."

We doff our caps and bow, and then scatter toward our bikes.

• • •

The next morning, when we run onto the field for pre-game practice, I see that the stadium bleachers are packed. I look up into the crowd and pick out my dad and my grandfather. I see lots of kids that I know from school, and a guy who looks like the coach of my elementary school baseball team.

We go through our usual drills, then Coach calls us back to the bench. The dugout is now decorated with hundreds of origami cranes, souvenirs from the last four teams we faced. We form a ring around the coach.

"Now remember," he says. "Just relax and play like you always do. Try to enjoy the game."

We all nod and say, *"Hai!"* But I can tell from

the way that Sagawa is twitching, and from the wrinkles on Kikawa's forehead that they are nervous. We're all nervous. It feels like there are frogs jumping around in my stomach.

"Okay, then," Coach says. "Go get 'em!"

The siren blares. We run onto the field, get into formation, and bow. Showtime! We're first at bat.

As the first guy steps up to the plate, the Hawks' pitcher reaches into his pocket, takes out a folded white handkerchief, and pats his forehead. Is that some kind of a sign? Is the hankie a good luck charm? Most guys would just drag a sleeve across their faces to sop up the sweat. Maybe he's just trying to distract the batters by being weird.

He puts the cloth back into his pocket and tosses the ball to Inoue. The first one goes by— high and outside—but Inoue takes a whack at the second pitch and sends it into left field.

A roar goes up from the crowd, and the brass band starts to play as Inoue makes it to first.

Next, Tanaka steps up to the plate. He glances over at Coach, who touches his cap, his chest, then his left shoulder. It seems a little early in the game to me for a sacrifice bunt, but Coach wants us to get a run as soon as possible.

Tanaka nods, and when the ball comes across the plate, he lays it down in the dirt and makes a mad dash for first. The pitcher rushes forward and scoops up the ball, fires it to first base. Tanaka is out, but Inoue has made it to second.

Sagawa, our short-stop, is third in the line-up today. He whiffs the first ball—a tricky slider—hits a couple of fouls, and then manages to put the ball into play. He's thrown out, but Inoue advances to third base.

Now we've got two outs, and a runner on third.

The pitcher takes off his cap, and pulls the handkerchief out of his pocket. Dab, dab, pat, pat. He tucks it back into his pocket, puts his cap back on, and bends down to grab a handful of chalk. Then he stands back up and stares down the line, fierce and stoic.

Noda, our center fielder, whose batting average is now at .400, raises his bat.

A loud ping rings out as the bat makes contact. The ball arcs into the air. The center fielder goes racing after it, but the ball misses his outstretched glove and thuds to the grass. Noda makes it to second, and Inoue crosses the plate.

We're off to a good start, but the Hawks catch

up in the next inning. By the time I get up to bat, the score is 2–2. We've got a runner on third, with two outs.

I wait at the plate, muscles tensed, while the pitcher dabs at his brow, and wonder again if that white handkerchief has any special meaning. I watch him tuck it back into his pocket, all properly, like a girl. I'm so caught up in thinking about that piece of cloth that my timing goes off. The first pitch sails right by.

"Strike one!"

I swear under my breath, then tense up again, determined to get a piece. There's a sweet spot in left field where no one is standing. I'm going to put the ball right there, in the grass, and run like the wind.

Sweat drips from my forehead, and dribbles down my back, but I ignore it. My eyes are on the ball as it leaves the pitcher's hand. I know it's a little high, but I take a swing anyway. I hear the ball pop in the catcher's mitt.

"Strike two!"

My hairline is itchy, but I can't scratch. I'm sweating more than ever, and it's not just the heavy July heat, but nerves and fear. My throat

is as dry as a desert. I've gotta put the ball into play. Everyone is depending on me—Takashima on third base, the guys in the dugout, my other teammates in the stands. I've gotta do this for my parents, for Oji-chan.

The pitcher winds up. His elbow pulls back, and then that white orb is flying toward me, hurtling like a meteor, and I swing again. Nothing. Not even a nick.

"Strike three. And you're out!"

The umpire's words are like a punch in my gut. I drag myself out of the batter's box, head down. I want to throw my helmet to the dusty ground, twist my aluminum bat into a pretzel. But of course, I don't.

Kikawa slaps my back. "Don't worry about it," he says. "Just think about the next inning."

I remind myself that Babe Ruth struck out 1,360 times. And Hank Aaron struck out 1,380 times. Even Ichiro had an off day once in a while.

I'm so parched, I'd almost give up my next turn at bat for a swig of water, but the other guys are already headed out to the field. That drink will have to wait. I scoop up my mitt from the bench and run out to right field.

The first batter up hits a line drive down the middle and is thrown out at first. The next guy pops up the ball—an easy out for Kikawa. But the third guy, their powerhouse, swings at an inside strike and sends it all the way over the wall. Home run. So now they're up 3–2 at the top of the third.

We get two outs in a row, and score again in the bottom of the third.

During my next at bat, I pop a fly to center.

The game goes back and forth, until we're

down 7–6 with only one inning to go.

At the top of the ninth, as I'm on deck warming up, I glance up at my parents and my grandfather in the stands. I rest my bat on my shoulder and scan the spectators again.

Wild applause breaks out. The sound jerks my attention back to the game. Abe has managed to get onto first. So now we have the tying runner on base, with one out. A victory, a championship, and a trip to the all-Japan tournament are within reach.

I take a deep breath, swing the bat a couple more times, tap twice on my helmet for good luck, and step up to the plate.

I glance over at the dugout. Coach touches the bill of his cap, his chest, his left shoulder. He wants me to bunt. A sacrifice bunt would move the runner to second, and then, with luck, the next batter could send him home. It's a cautious move.

"Baseball is a game of probability," Coach always says. Probably the runner will make it to second if I bunt well. But if I swing, anything could happen.

I nod, and wait for the pitch. It comes flying, high and outside. I let it go. Ball one.

And then, I look up to my left, and there's Oji-chan. He's wearing a cap and an old Peace Junior High School jersey, leaning over the rail as if he's trying to tell me something. I can't see his eyes, but I know he's watching me, waiting for me to be a hero instead of the wimpy guy who can't stand up for himself. I can hit the ball. I'll show him what I can do.

When that ball comes across the plate, I'll swing like Hank Aaron. Like Ichiro. I'll blast that ball into space. It'll be like the Hornets vs. Bobcats all over again, this time on Japanese soil. I'll win this game and take us to the National Tournament. I'll save the team. Top high school and college coaches and pro scouts will come calling. And Oji-chan will be amazed.

I look into the pitcher's eyes, see the determination there. We scowl at each other for a moment, and then he goes into his wind-up.

The ball comes shooting toward me. I swing.

23

P*ing!* The ball goes flying. I drop the bat and make a mad dash for first, legs churning, arms pumping. Out of the corner of my eye, I see the shortstop running to catch the ball. Then I hear the smack as it falls into his glove. I'm out.

Abe is midway between bases. He turns back, but the shortstop fires the ball to the first baseman. Now he's trapped between the two of them. He tries to veer around the first baseman, but it's no use. The other player reaches and tags him.

"Out!" the umpire yells.

The outfielders swarm to the center of the diamond, and the Hawks' players start hugging each other, pounding each other on the back. They lift their champion pitcher into the air. Applause rises from the bleachers.

What have I done? I can hardly drag myself back to the dugout.

When I get there, I see that my teammates are crying. They're sobbing. Tanaka is howling, snot coming out of his nose. Kikawa's face is streaked with tears. I feel a burning at the back of my eyeballs, but I can't cry in front of all of these people. There's still an echo of Coach Harris' voice in my head: "If you're going to lose, do it with grace. I don't want any sore losers on my team." I bite down on my lips and turn away from my wailing teammates.

We still have to go out onto the field and bow to the guys who beat us. Coach allows us a few minutes to compose ourselves, and tells us to line up. We run out, get into formation and bow.

The guy across from me is grinning, probably doing all he can to keep from leaping across the field. I look down at the dirt, at my scuffed-up shoes, and then shuffle off the field.

I hear a low voice behind me. *"Traitor!"*

I blink back tears. If only I could turn back the hands of time and bunt! If only I could spontaneously combust or disappear!

We're mostly silent in the locker room, and on

the bus back to school. People avoid me like I've got the zombie plague. I sit by myself and stare out the window. The seat next to mine is empty. I can feel the anger and blame coming from the other players like a wave.

• • •

Back at school, just before the post mortem, Coach hangs his head for a moment and says, "I know it hurts to lose, but you have nothing to be ashamed of." He looks each player in the eyes— everyone but me—and says a few more words about the team's fighting spirit, the improvements we've made over the season, and good wishes for the future. The third-year students are now finished with junior high school baseball. They'll have to wait until after graduation to play on a team again, if ever.

Coach isn't the only one giving me the cold shoulder. The other guys avoid looking at me as well. Only Junji bothers to speak to me at all. "You messed up, bro," he says, punching my shoulder. "It's gonna take a lot of laps around the field before Coach forgives you. *A lot* of laps."

I try to swallow the lump in my throat, but it's

stuck there, seemingly for eternity.

"Hey, guys, wanna go get some ramen?" Kikawa asks.

Some of the guys grunt and nod. I don't say anything. I don't feel exactly welcome.

Coach motions me over to him. "So what happened out there?" he asks.

"I didn't bunt," I say. Shame washes through me.

He nods. "You ignored me, didn't you? If you're not going to respect me, then don't bother coming to practice. Go find another team."

"*Wakarimashita,*" I say. *I understand.* So that's it, then. I'm banned. I'm off the team. My life is over.

He turns away from me and goes into the club house.

This has to be the worst day of my life. And now I have to walk past the other players to get to my bike. What'll I tell my parents? What'll I say to Oji-chan? How am I going to explain that his greatest wish has no chance of coming true?

Shintaro leans toward me and says in a low voice, "So you're a retard, just like your sister, huh? Can't remember the signs?"

His words light a fuse inside of me and... detonate! I have nothing to lose. I'm already off the team. Chances are, this team won't make it to the finals. There will be no more baseball at Tokushima Whirlpool Junior High School. No more baseball for me, ever. If I get into a fight, so what? Maybe Shintaro will get kicked off, too. I pull my arm back and swing. This time I connect—my fist, and his nose. Crunch!

"Owwww!"

Blood comes gushing out of his nose. But here's the thing: the rage welling up inside me is pushing out every other emotion. I don't feel sad about losing. I don't feel lonely about being left out of their plans. But the feeling doesn't last long.

Just when I'm starting to wonder when he's going to hit me back, I hear, "Matsumoto!" It's Coach.

At the sound of his voice, I remember a speech he gave about a month ago about how one person's behavior affects the whole team. If any of us gets into a fight, Coach will have to report it and the team won't be able to play in the next tournament. This won't be good. *"Hai?"*

The other players step back. The manager, who

must have seen the whole thing, comes rushing up to Shintaro with a box of tissues and some ice cubes wrapped in a handkerchief. She starts cooing like a nurse. Then they all seem to fade away as Coach steps forward.

His face is hard. "What's going on here?"

"I bumped my nose," Shintaro says. "Satoshi here was trying to help."

Coach stares at us for a moment. I don't know if he believes Shintaro or not, but we both put on our most innocent faces, and he finally nods. "Keep it iced," he says, and then he walks away again.

"I'm going to get you for that," Shintaro says under his breath.

And now I really do feel like throwing up.

24

I'm alone. Totally. I feel as if all of the air has gone out of me. As if I'm the one who's been punched. In the gut. What now? I could go home to Oji-chan's sad face, and my mother's sympathy. I could go to a game center and try to lose my misery in pinball, or down to the riverbank to throw rocks into the water. Nah.

And then I catch a flash of pink at the corner of my eye. I turn to see Misa, standing there with her sunglasses pushed on top of her head, her hands knotted behind her back. Seeing her makes me feel mad all over again.

"Why did you have to go and tell everyone about my sister?" It must have been her. Who else would have blabbed?

"I... I..." Her mouth hangs open for a moment. Tears fill her eyes and her shoulders slump.

Finally, she gives up, turns away, and runs in the other direction. I realize that I officially have no more friends here.

At home, no one mentions the game. My mother and father tiptoe around me as if they're afraid I might explode. Even Momoko seems to sense that something happened. She pats me on the back as I walk past her.

I eat dinner with my family, then hole up in my room to listen to music and surf the Internet. I dash off a message to Rico and Jamal: "Hey, how are things in Atlanta? I miss playing baseball with you guys!"

I figure they're still snoozing, since it's morning over there and summer vacation has already started, but there's a reply from Rico almost immediately: "Dude! Wait till you meet my new girlfriend!" I quickly glance over the rest of the message. Jamal broke his arm skateboarding, so he's out of commission for a while. Both of them will be taking driver's ed later this summer. There's nothing about the team or about baseball.

Before I go to bed, I make sure to turn off the alarm on my clock. I'm not going to practice tomorrow, so I can sleep in.

All night long, I dream of that final pitch coming toward me. Every time I hit it, the same thing happens. When I finally drag myself out of bed at ten thirty a.m., I find the newspaper on the kitchen table. "Tokushima Hawks Win!" the headline blares above a photo of the team hugging each other.

I ought to turn away, but I can't help myself. I open the newspaper to the centerfold which is devoted to yesterday's game. There are several stories, and several photos, all in color. The images are mostly of Tokusho's players at various moments of triumph, but there's also one of me swinging the bat in the ninth inning. And another of my teammates hanging their heads and wiping their eyes. I'm in the corner of that picture looking a little pissed, but I'm not crying and my back is straight. I don't look sorry. I don't even look like a good sport. Everyone must think I'm a total jerk.

My mother comes into the kitchen just then. "Do you want me to make you some breakfast?"

"Nah, that's okay. I'm not hungry."

She nods. "Maybe you could go over and visit Oji-chan for a while. I need to run a few errands."

"Sure." I have nowhere else to go.

I open the refrigerator, grab a carton of orange juice, and guzzle it down. Then I change into baggy shorts and my Atlanta Braves T-shirt and head over to Oji-chan's.

"Ohayo gozaimasu!" I say, sliding open the door.

"Ohayo, Satoshi."

Well, at least he knows who I am today.

The TV's on and he's sitting there in his undershirt with a glass of cold barley tea, Nana-chan at his side. The windows are open, and there's a bit of a breeze, tinkling the wind chimes hanging above the sink.

"That was too bad yesterday," Oji-chan says.

"Yeah." *You have no idea.* "So how's Nana-chan doing?" I ask, trying to change the subject.

He chuckles. "She's fine."

"Must be hot with all that fur," I say.

He's silent for a moment. Then he says, "I don't understand why Coach Ogawa didn't tell you to bunt. That would have been my move."

At any other time, I would be happy to see him so lucid, but right now I'm kind of wishing he was lost in the past. I'm too ashamed to say that I disobeyed. And there's no way that I can tell him

I've been kicked off the team, no way that I can tell him that the baseball team may not even exist next year.

"Aren't you supposed to be at practice now?" Oji-chan asks.

"Yeah," I lie. "I need to go now."

I bike over to Major Sports and hit ball after ball until my arms feel like wet ramen noodles and then I retreat home, my secret grinding me into the ground.

25

The team captain communicates with everybody by listserv. No one remembers at first to remove me from the list, so I get all of the messages about practice times, and whose turn it is to bring raw rice for making rice balls for the afternoon snack. I get the message announcing that Shintaro Nakamoto is the new team captain, now that the third-year students have retired in order to study for high school entrance exams. Even though I get the messages, I don't go to practice. Obviously.

Okaasan doesn't say anything about my new routine at first, but on about day nine, a Saturday, when Otosan is home for the weekend and I'm in my room playing a video game, there's a knock on the door.

"Come in," I yell.

My bedroom door creaks open and my mother

steps into the room. "Your father and I want to have a talk with you," she says.

I'm on the verge of obliterating my previous high score, only two more zombies to go, but I shrug. "Yeah, sure."

Okaasan hesitates for a moment. "We'll be waiting at the kitchen table."

I wait until she has left my room and closed the door. I listen to her footsteps receding down the hallway, down the stairs, and then I sigh and log off the computer.

My father and mother are sitting at the table, their foreheads creased with worry. There are three glasses of tea set out—one in front of each of them, and one at my place. I sit down and take a gulp.

Otosan clears his throat and begins. "We've noticed that you stopped going to baseball practice."

"Yeah." My stomach knots up. I feel a pang in my chest. "I got kicked off the team."

They exchange looks. My mother sucks in her breath.

"Why?" Otosan asks.

I shrug. "Coach told me to bunt, and I ignored him. I thought I could hit the ball and win the game. I was wrong. I got kicked off the team."

My father is silent. He shakes his head, as if he can't believe what he's hearing.

"Did you make an apology?" my mother asks. "Maybe if you showed Coach Ogawa that you were sorry, and how much you wanted to play, he'd let you back on the team."

"Yeah, maybe," I say. "But there's more. I got into a fight with Shintaro Nakamoto."

My father looks up, suddenly alert. His face has gone pale. "Nakamoto? The bar owner's son?"

Okaasan's jaw drops. "Of all people..."

Okaasan and Otosan exchange a look. Obviously, they know all about the Nakamoto family. They remember the rumors. Maybe they know things that even I don't know.

"Nakamoto," Otosan murmurs. "Yeah, you'd better stay away from him."

I don't bother telling them that he's the new team captain.

In the days that follow, I don't say anything to Oji-chan about my exile from the baseball team. He still doesn't know a thing two weeks later when we turn on the TV to watch the opening ceremony of the National High School Tournament at Koshien. Oji-chan hasn't asked me why I haven't been going to baseball practice either, which is just as well.

"How's your friend?" he asks.

"Misa?" I'm pretty sure she's not my friend anymore, but he doesn't need to know that. "Uh, good. She's been too busy to hang out." This seems to satisfy him. He doesn't say anything else about her.

On TV, the winning teams from all forty-seven prefectures of Japan march into the stadium and take their places on the field. It's blistering out there, but they stand perfectly still, waiting for everyone to line up.

Tokushima Prefecture's team appears about midway. When they march into the stadium, I feel a mixture of pride and regret. I can't help thinking about my team. I still wish I could go back in time and change the outcome of that last game.

When they've reached the podium, the players salute the Crown Prince who is way up high—as high as you can go—in the bleachers. Then they go out onto the field.

After everyone has assembled, the speeches begin. The head of the baseball association delivers opening remarks, then the captain of last year's championship team says a few words. Finally, the Crown Prince greets the crowd from his uppermost place in the stands. He speaks about watching the tournament at Koshien as a boy, about how excited he was, and how much he looks forward to the games even now. Closing remarks are made and then the ceremony is finished. Forty-seven teams march off the grounds in perfect formation and the first two teams to play take to the field for preliminary practice.

Oji-chan's eyes shine. "One day I'll see you on that field. That will be a happy day," he says.

I'm not sure if he's talking to his son, Masahiro, or his grandson, me. "Yeah," I murmur. "It'll be great." My gut twists inside.

The camera pans over the crowd—55,000 people, the announcer says. Many spectators have towels draped around their necks or over their heads. Paper fans are flapping. Some people are eating shaved ice. It must be such a high to play on that field with all of those people watching and cheering.

The whirr of helicopter blades comes from the TV. Game time. The two teams—one from Okinawa, one from Saitama, are now in position to play. The chopper hovers over the stadium and a brand-new ball is dropped from the sky. It parachutes gently to the center of the diamond, and the tournament begins.

Oji-chan and I sit in his air-conditioned room with our cold tea. It's comfortable, but part of me wishes I were there, in the heat, amidst the buzz of excitement. But then I forget where I am, and get into the game.

The pitcher from Okinawa is really good. He has a side-winding throw that's hard to hit. He strikes out two batters in a row. The third one pops up an infield fly. The pitcher catches it and makes the third out.

Saitama's pitcher isn't bad either. The two teams seem pretty evenly matched. By the end of the seventh inning, the score is 0–0. But then at the bottom of the eighth, the center fielder fumbles a fly, committing the first error of the game.

Oji-chan shakes his head and sucks his teeth. "The spirits at Koshien don't like to see careless mistakes on the field," he says.

And maybe he's right, because with two on base, the third batter on the Okinawa team hits a home run. The applause is deafening.

"See? What did I tell you?" Oji-chan says, happy to see some action.

On the TV screen, there's a close-up of the runner's face as he crosses home plate. His teeth are brilliant against his tanned face. He can't stop smiling. His teammates are raising their arms in triumph. I feel a sense of envy.

I wonder if any of the guys on this team will go pro. Scouts are in the stands with their clipboards, taking notes on their favorite players. Next year, the best players from this tournament will show up in the J-League or maybe even the Majors.

The game ends with the team from Okinawa in the lead, 1–0. The teams line up and bow to each other. Of course, the guys from Saitama are in tears. They hurry off the field, drop to their knees and start clawing at the earth, scooping up handfuls of dirt and filling plastic bags with it. It's a tradition to take home dirt from Koshien as a souvenir. It's proof that you were there.

"Do you know about Shuri High School?" Oji-chan asks.

"In Okinawa?" I ask.

"Yes. They were the first team from Okinawa to play in the national tournament, back when the islands were under American control."

"What happened?"

"Well, they lost in the first game, and they took some dirt back with them to remember their time at Koshien, but it was confiscated at the airport. They didn't want anyone bringing foreign soil into the islands. It might have alien insects or something."

No team from Okinawa has ever won the national summer tournament at Koshien, although the Okinawa Fisheries High School was runner-up twice, back in the 1990s. Although I should be loyal to the team from Tokushima, I sort of hope the Okinawa team wins. *"Ganbare,"* I say under my breath.

• • •

Watching all those bats swinging makes me twitchy. Time for me to go to batting practice.

"I'm going to Major Sports," I shout out to my mother.

"Be home in time for dinner," she calls back. "And pick up some milk on the way."

As soon as I walk in the door, I see Shintaro. *Great.* He's looking the other way, so I ease slowly, quietly, back out the door. I catch a glimpse of his nose. It looks okay, so I guess I didn't break it.

I decide that I'll come back later and hit some balls when the coast is clear. It's not until I'm once again on my bicycle that I think to wonder what he's doing there. He's the new team captain. Why isn't he at school, practicing with the rest of the team? Could he be on academic probation or something? I remember how he got his test back last in English, how he balled it up and tossed it in the trash.

Wow. I bet his dad will kill him if he gets kicked off the team. My mind flashes to an image of Shintaro's father, fingers hooked through the chain link fence like a tiger, cursing under his breath. I picture his big paw swiping the side of Shintaro's face.

But I know that he doesn't play only because he's afraid of his father. I know Shintaro truly loves baseball. Even when we were little kids, he'd spend hours pitching against a brick wall. I used to see him every time I came to Major Sports. Plus, he wouldn't have cut his hair if he wasn't serious. He wouldn't have written that stupid essay. He wouldn't have kept his fists to himself and lied about how he got a bloody nose even though I know he wanted to punch me back. He hasn't missed a practice ever. I know he doesn't want to quit.

"That sucks," I say to myself. Without a decent pitcher, there's no way the team can win. Now that Kikawa is a third-year student and had to quit baseball to study for high school entrance exams, Shintaro's the best they've got.

27

The next evening I spend a couple of hours at Major Sports. Swing! The ball torpedoes. Whoosh! Over the fence. By the time I'm finished, I'm exhausted, but it's a good kind of tired.

It's dark when I hop on my bike and start for home. I pedal slowly. Just as I reach the temple, I nearly collide with three murky figures blocking my path. "Hey, watch out!" I say, skidding to a stop.

Someone grabs onto my handlebars. And then somebody else is yanking on my shoulders, pulling me off the bike. I stumble, almost losing my balance. My bicycle crashes to the ground.

"Hello, Satoshi." Shintaro steps out of the shadows. His voice is low and menacing. He's holding an aluminum bat against his shoulder.

He and his goons are in street clothes. They definitely don't look like they're on their way to a baseball game. The other guys aren't even on the team—at least not at our school.

Before I can make sense of what's happening, the two guys that I don't know grab my arms and pin them behind my back. I try to jerk away, but they hold me tighter. Shintaro swaggers closer and gets into batting position.

I may be done with fighting, but it looks like fighting is not done with me.

"This is for punching me in front of the team," he says.

For a second, I imagine my head blasted into space, an out-of-the-park homerun. If I wasn't so scared, I might laugh at that.

"W-wait!"

He sneers. "Wait for what?"

"Th-think about what you're doing. You'll get kicked off the team for beating me up. Coach is gonna find out, one way or another."

"Haven't you heard?" He steps away and takes a warm-up swing that stops just in front of my nose. "I already got kicked off because of my grades. And the coach is gone."

What? My heart is pounding like a *taiko* drum. If these guys weren't holding my arms up, I think

I'd keel over in fright. They are stronger than me. There's no way I can break free. And even if I did, they would still be after me, endlessly seeking revenge. Enough. I shouldn't have hit him. I shouldn't have hit that ball. I deserve all this and more. I close my eyes and prepare to meet my fate.

I hear the bat slicing through air and then— *whack!* My rear end suddenly feels like it's burst into flames. Man, that hurt! Stars are spinning around my head and when I open my eyes, I can hardly see straight. But I'm not bleeding. And I'm not crying. As far as I can tell, nothing is broken.

It's over, I think, and I'm still alive! But then out of the corner of my eye, I see Shintaro poised to take another swing.

"Wait!" I manage to blurt out. "I can help you."

The guys holding my arms snicker, but Shintaro seems ready to listen. "How so?"

"I-I'll give you the answers during our next English test." There's going to be a big test the first week back at school, the one that will determine whether he'll be able to play in the fall tournament. If he passes that, he can get back on the team.

"How are you going to do that?" he demands. "You sit way up in front. I'm in the back."

Quick! I have to come up with something. Origami German shepherds? Flying paper airplanes? And then it comes to me. "Tanaka's tests are always multiple choice, right? We'll work out a system. I can give you signs."

Shintaro finally lowers the bat and nods to his friends. They let go of my arms. One guy shoves me, so that I fall to the pavement. I lie there with my eyes closed until I hear them stomp off into the night.

28

When I hobble into the house about an hour later, I find Misa sitting at the kitchen table playing cards with Momoko. My mom isn't around.

Momoko is smiling and happy for once. I feel bad that she's been lonely because of me, because I didn't want Misa to come and hang out with her. Suddenly I don't care anymore whether or not she told everyone about Momoko. Just when I'm about to apologize to her, Misa speaks up.

"I never told anyone about your sister," she says.

"Huh. I wonder how Shintaro found out?"

"I heard Junji talking about her once. He saw you with her at the mall."

Figures. Oh, well. Now that the truth is out, I have nothing to hide.

She suddenly notices that I'm all roughed up. "What happened to you?" Her voice goes soft.

"Shintaro," I say.

It's enough. She understands. "Are you hurt?"

Definitely. More than hurt. I am pain itself. I don't think I'll ever be able to sit down again. "I'm okay."

In spite of the ache, I feel relief. The dread that has been nagging at me since I punched Shintaro, that has been giving me nightmares and twisting my stomach, is gone. I figure we're even. We don't have to be friends, but I know that the baseball team can't win without him. If they don't win, it'll be all twirling ribbons and lacrosse sticks from here on out. My grandfather's legacy will be history. I have to figure out a way to get Shintaro back on the team.

• • •

It's not until the next afternoon that I remember the other problem. Coach is gone. What exactly did Shintaro mean by that? Is he on vacation or something? Was he fired? I'm lying in my bed on my stomach with a pack of frozen peas on my butt. I thumb a quick text to Junji. He might know what's going on. And yes, a few seconds later *ping*! I get a reply.

"He quit," Junji texts back. "Baseball is over."

That's crazy. I reach up and touch my head. My hair is longer, like bristles on a brush. I think it's time for another *bozu*. Those guys at the barber shop might know what's going on.

I remove the peas and carefully get out of bed. I find my Mom downstairs, helping my sister with her daily exercises. Momoko is on a mat, and Okaasan is stretching her legs so she doesn't get all folded up.

"Can I have some money for a haircut?" I ask her.

She frowns. "I thought you weren't on the team anymore."

"I still love baseball," I say. And I do! Getting my hair shaved off is my way of showing my devotion to the game. I'm not giving up on our team. And I need to know what happened to the coach.

She nods and doesn't ask any more questions. "You can take a thousand yen out of my purse."

"Thanks." I grab the money and set off my bicycle. It hurts to sit on the saddle, so I ride while standing most of the way.

The barber looks up from shaving another customer when I walk in the door. "Hey, there," he says. "Aren't you that kid from the Whirlpool

Junior High School team?"

"Yes," I say. And sure enough, these guys have intel.

"Heard that Nakamoto boy got kicked off the team for bad grades and his father threatened to beat up the coach," the guy in the chair says through the foam on his face.

"He was in here for a haircut last week," the barber says. "He said he had an offer to coach the team at some international school in Kobe. They start the semester in September, like the American schools."

So that's what happened. With Shintaro and me off the team, maybe Coach figured they'd lose in the next tournament and he'd be out of a job anyway. And if Nakamoto's dad was angry with him, well, considering what his son did to my rear end, I wouldn't blame him for leaving.

I stand around waiting until the barber finishes shaving the other guy, then I take a deep breath and sit in the chair. Ooh, it hurts to sit, but I don't even wince. "Give me a *bozu*," I say. Whirlpool Junior High baseball is not over yet. I'll find a way to save the team.

It's been awhile since I got a message on

the listserv. I figured that my address had been deleted, but when I post a message—"Testing! Testing!"—it doesn't bounce back. I post another "Keep practicing baseball! Remember the *ronin*!" We learned about *ronin* in school. There was a movie, too, and a whole manga series. They were samurai warriors who had lost their masters. They banded together and won battles. We can do the same. If we unite as a team, we can win games, even the tournament, whether we have a coach or not. And if we win, the school owner will have to take notice and keep the team.

"Where can we practice?" Junji texts back. "The principal says we can't use the baseball diamond. If someone gets injured during practice, and there's no one in charge, the school could get in trouble."

"Go to Major Sports then," I text back. "Find a way!"

Later that day, I ride my bike to school, thinking that being there will give me some ideas. I expect to see an empty outfield, but there are a bunch of students waving around long sticks with basket-like things on the ends. They're trying to pass a ball to each other. There's a guy in shorts

I've never seen before. He blows a whistle, and everyone stops moving to listen.

I suddenly realize that they are trying to play lacrosse. The changeover has already begun.

We need a place to practice together, and we need a new coach. And somehow we need to get Nakamoto back on the team. Even if he is a jerk, he's still our best pitcher. All of the teachers are too busy to take over responsibility for coaching, and none of them really knows about baseball. Maybe Oji-chan could help out, when his mind isn't in the last century, but knowing that this team is about to be demolished would probably destroy him as well.

29

It takes about a week for the bruises to heal. On the first morning that I can finally sit down without remembering how that bat felt across my butt, I catch Okaasan in her apron. "I'm off to my French cooking lesson," she says. "We're making crème brulee today."

"Bring back some for us," I say, my mouth starting to water. Last week they made some sort of apple pie.

"So, you'll be around to look after Oji-chan, right?"

Momoko is at school, checking in with her teachers. That's one thing about school in Japan— even when you're on "vacation," there are still all kinds of extra classes.

"Yeah, we're going to watch baseball together. Just us guys."

She jingles her keys for a moment, hesitating.

"Go ahead." I shoo her out the door. "Have fun! We'll be fine. I'll make us some noodles."

Ramen is about the only thing I know how to cook. I grab some cabbage and carrots out of the crisper, chop up the vegetables, and get a pot of water boiling. I toss in dried noodles and the vegetables, and break a couple of eggs into the broth. *Et voila.* I arrange two bowls of soup on a tray with some chopsticks and bring it over to Oji-chan's house.

"Ramen!" he says. "I used to make that for your dad."

"Really?" I've always been under the impression that they didn't do much together. I'm glad that I was wrong.

We slurp our noodles while watching baseball on TV. Just watching makes me want to swing a bat. I look over at my grandfather. He's pretty engrossed in the game. I could probably slip away for an hour or so and get some practice in. And maybe I could invite Misa to come, too.

"Want to hit some balls at Major Sports in one hour?" I text.

She answers almost right away: "Okay!"

After our bowls are drained, I wipe the table and wash the dishes. When I turn back to Oji-chan, I see that he's nodded off. His head is cradled in his arms and he's snoring gently. Perfect.

Nana-chan is moving around a little more slowly than usual. I guess her batteries will need recharging soon. I can do that when I get back. Later on, Oji-chan and I will watch that team from Okinawa play in the next round, but for now, I've got enough time to put in a little batting practice. With any luck, I'll be back before he wakes up. I leave him a note anyway.

Misa's already waiting when I get there. She leans against the wall, just to the left of the door, shading her eyes against the sun.

"What's with the mini skirt?" I tease. "We're baseball players, not pom pom girls."

She sticks her tongue out at me and follows me inside.

The batting center is empty this time of day. I go into the cage with my bat and take my position. When the ball comes, I swing as if it matters.

Misa doesn't say anything as she takes the bat from me. She lines up in front of the base, lofts the bat into the air, and waits. When the pitch comes, she takes a wild swing and misses.

"You've got to keep your eye on the ball," I tell her.

She swings at the next pitch, and this time connects. The ball flies into what would be center field if this were a real ball park. When she turns to me, her eyes are suddenly alight with hope.

30

We're having such a good time that I forget to look at my watch. When I finally do, I realize that the game with the team from Okinawa has already started. Oji-chan is probably awake. "Oh, no. I have to get back. Do you want to come over and watch the school baseball tournament on TV with Oji-chan and me?"

She shrugs. "Sure."

We go back out into the heat of the day.

At home, Misa waits in the kitchen while I grab a big bottle of Pocari Sweat from the refrigerator and a bag of dried squid for snacking on, and we head over to Oji-chan's quarters.

He's not there. The TV is on, tuned to the baseball game at Koshien. A glass of tea is sitting on the low table, the ice cubes half-melted. He must have woken up from his nap just a little while ago.

I turn off the TV and stand there, listening. Something's not quite right. It's too quiet. It takes me a minute to figure it out. *Nana-chan*. Normally, she'd be yipping or flopping around the room. I check in the entryway, and the closet, but she's not there. And neither is Oji-chan.

"I'll look around outside," Misa says.

"Thanks. I'm going to check our house." *Okay, be calm*, I tell myself. He's not in the bathroom, or in any of the other rooms in our house. I peer into the shed where my mother keeps her potting soil and gardening tools. And then I take a walk around the neighborhood, hoping I'll come across someone who's seen him. But it's too hot to be outside. It's way too hot. I read in the newspaper that over the past two weeks two hundred people have died from heat stroke—mostly elderly people who have a hard time regulating their body temperatures and don't want to use air-conditioning. Oji-chan should be in the cool, in the shade.

"Any luck?" Misa asks, as she comes around the corner.

"No." Maybe he went looking for Okaasan. "Could you ride your bike over to the Community Center? My mom's at her cooking lesson. Maybe he's on the way there."

"Sure thing." She sprints around the corner.

I run home, pull a cap onto my head, and hop on my bike.

Today the cemetery is empty. Oji-chan's not anywhere nearby. He's not wandering down the little lanes near the house, and he isn't along the rice paddies. At the side of the road I put my elbows on the handlebars of my bicycle and rest my head in my hands for a moment. Where else could he be? I reach into my pocket and touch my cell phone, wonder if I should make a call. But wait—there's one more place that I need to check before I involve the volunteer fire department.

The baseball field. I remember how he suddenly showed up at practice that one afternoon. Maybe he's at the junior high school now, looking for me.

I take a deep breath. I don't really want to run into the lacrosse team again, but I've got to find Oji-chan, and he's as likely to be at a baseball field as anywhere else. I have no choice but to go there.

I take a swig of water. *Okay, here I go.*

I'm hoping that no one will be there, except for my grandfather of course. Maybe they've already had practice this morning. No such luck. When I pull up on my bike at about three o'clock in the afternoon, I see that they are just setting up.

I stand near the chain link fence, trying to scope out the field without being seen, but someone yells out, "Hey, Matsumoto!" and everyone turns to look.

I raise my hand in a feeble salute.

Junji dashes over. Amazingly, he's smiling, as if he's happy to see me. Then again, maybe he's just happy. "What are you doing here?" I ask. "You're not joining the lacrosse team, are you?"

He looks down. "It's actually pretty fun. Do you want to try?"

"Naw," I say. "I'm looking for my grandfather. He wandered away again and I thought he might be here."

"What's going on?" The lacrosse coach swaggers up behind Junji. His eyes are hidden behind dark glasses. He seems annoyed, but listens carefully as Junji explains the situation.

"Can I help him look?" Junji asks.

"Your choice," the coach says. "If you want to be on the lacrosse team, you stay. If not..."

Junji looks back at the guys with the baskets on sticks, seems to think for a moment, then nods.

"Okay. I'm going with Satoshi."

I grab my phone and thumb a text to the baseball team listserv. "My grandfather is missing! Please help me look for him!" Then I hope for the best.

31

"**G**ot any ideas?" Junji asks.

I shrug. "I thought he'd be here. Maybe he got on a bus or something?"

Junji is silent for a moment, biting his lip. "Hey, did you go by Aizumi Primary?" he asks, referring to our old elementary school.

I shake my head.

"Let's go check it out," Junji says. "Your grandfather used to go to all of our games. Maybe that's where he went."

"It's worth a try," I say. We take off, Junji in the lead.

There are a couple of cars in the Aizumi Primary School parking lot, but the baseball diamond out back is empty. I crouch down in the dirt, suddenly overcome with fatigue.

"Hey, look who's here!" Junji says.

Shintaro pulls up on his bicycle. He sends up a shower of pebbles when he suddenly stops. "I got your message," he says. "I remember how your grandfather used to come here to watch our elementary school games. Good times."

Junji and I look at each other. Who knew Shintaro could care about other people? And that he had happy memories of playing with us?

Shintaro whips out his thermos. "Want some?" he asks.

Sweat is dribbling down my forehead. My shirt is soaked through. For all I know, he's offering me a swig of battery acid. But, dang, I'm thirsty. "Thanks." I pour some cold tea down my throat and hand the thermos back.

"Man, it's so hot," Junji says. "I wish I could just jump in the river."

My head jerks up. *The river.* That's it! "Come on, you guys. I think I know where he is."

I hop back on my bike and pedal furiously. I don't even check to see if Shintaro and Junji are following me. Everything is a blur until I get to the riverbank, throw my bike down on the grass, and run down the hill.

My heart almost stops when I see him. He's

standing out on a sand bar, holding that damn robot seal. The tide is coming in, so the water's already at his waist.

"Oji-chan!" I yell. "Don't move!"

His head turns at the sound of my voice. He totters for a moment, then regains his balance. I've got to get out there, and fast. I take off my shoes and my shirt, and try to make a plan in my head. The current is strong here. If Oji-chan panics, he could take us both under. I need a life preserver. A rope. Or even a long stick. But there's nothing on the shore.

"How'd he get out there?" Junji is behind me now, breathing heavily.

"I guess he waded out when the tide was down," I say. "Hey," I say, an idea forming. "Text the rest of the team and ask them to come over here."

I wade into the water. "Stay calm, Oji-chan. I'm here and more help is on the way."

He doesn't respond. I wonder if he's in shock, or if he's had a stroke or something. Maybe he's just too scared to speak. Well, maybe telling some stories will soothe him.

"Remember that game where our team was behind ten to zero in the sixth inning? Remember how everyone thought it would be called in the seventh?" I keep talking, giving him the play by play, until my teammates appear. I hear the squeak of bicycle brakes, excited voices, and the pound of running feet.

I turn and reach out my hand. Junji grabs on, and Shintaro grabs onto his other hand. Our human chain becomes longer and longer. I take a step toward Oji-chan, and they all follow me. We move slowly, but steadily, against the tide until I'm within reach of Oji-chan.

He is trembling now. And he's still holding that stupid Nana-chan.

"Let go of her," I shout. "Take my hand." He glances at me, his face full of fear, but he won't let go of the robot.

"She wasn't moving..." His words are mumbled, but they carry on the breeze.

Suddenly, I get it. Nana-chan's batteries wore down, and he thought the water would perk her up. He must have forgotten about her charger. Maybe he got the idea from seeing that show about real seals on TV.

"Let her swim away," I shout. "Let her find her friends! It's time for Nana-chan to be with her own

kind. You have your own kind, too. You have your family. Otosan, Okaasan, Momoko. And me!"

Just then he stumbles and falls face first into the water. I dive forward. I try to break free of Junji's hand, but he hangs on. Something slithers over my bare chest. The muddy water makes my eyes sting, but I can't close them. I can see Nana-chan sinking, and Oji-chan under the water, his limbs flailing. I catch his hand and pull him to me. And then we all drag my grandfather through the deep water, into the shallows.

When he's out of danger, Junji and Shintaro help me carry him onto the bank. He's coughing and sputtering, but I think he'll be okay. Even so, I grab my cell phone and call an ambulance, and then I call my parents to let them know that he's safe.

Then, suddenly overcome with exhaustion, Shintaro, Junji, and the rest of the guys and I collapse on the grass, and listen for the siren. Our sopping clothes are in a tangled pile. We're sitting here in our underwear, all muddy and wet. Leaves are sticking to my hair. We look ridiculous. I start to laugh, and pretty soon, Shintaro and Junji are laughing, too.

32

Oji-chan has to spend a night at the hospital under observation. Back at home, we have a family meeting with my father via webcam.

"I'm really sorry I left him alone," I say. Lately, all I seem to do is apologize. "I promise I'll never do it again."

I'm afraid that this will turn into another discussion about putting Oji-chan in a nursing home, but Otosan rubs his eyes under his glasses and says, "You should apologize for troubling your teammates and do something to thank them."

I know that it's the right thing to do. And I've got an idea of how I can pay them back.

• • •

The next morning, I put on my school uniform and bike to school. Even though it's still summer vacation, some teachers are there supervising club activities or preparing their lessons for the next semester. And the principal? Well, he's in his air-conditioned office every day. I go straight to the office and make an appointment to see him.

The office lady smiles at me like I'm a little kid. "Okay, you can go in now. Keep it short, though. He's a busy man."

I knock on the heavy wooden door.

"Enter!" Principal Mori calls out in his gruff voice.

I open the door, pause, and bow. *"Shitsurei shimasu!"*

He nods and waves me in impatiently. "Have a seat, Satoshi."

I perch on the edge of the black leather sofa that stretches in front of his desk. To my surprise, the door opens once again. The office lady appears with two small glasses of cold tea. She sets one on a coaster in front of Principal Mori, who grunts by way of thanks, and another on the long, low table in front of me. I'm thirsty, but I know better than to gulp it down.

"Well, then. Out with it," Principal Mori says.

"I'm sorry for bothering you, sir, but I would like to ask for permission to use the baseball field for team practice."

He sighs. "Well, you no longer have a coach, do you?"

"What if I can arrange for a new coaching team?"

Principal Mori is silent. He stares out at the window, out at the now-empty baseball diamond. He chuckles at some memory, and takes a noisy slurp of tea. "It would be a shame to lose our baseball team, wouldn't it?" he finally says. "But you do know that if the team doesn't perform well in the fall tournament, that there will be no more baseball after this."

"Yes, sir. I've heard that," I say. "Just give us one more chance."

He sighs again, drains his cup, and nods. "The lacrosse team is using the field in the afternoons. You can use it in the morning, provided you are properly supervised."

"Thank you, sir!" I rise, go to the doorway, and bow once again before making my exit.

"Oh, and Satoshi?"

"Yes?"

"Good luck," Principal Mori says.

Now that we've got a place to practice, we need a coach. I sent a text to Mr. Jerry. "Hi! I've got a big favor to ask you..."

33

After Oji-chan is released from the hospital, Okaasan drops us off at the baseball diamond with a watermelon as a token of our appreciation. A piece of fruit is hardly enough to thank them for helping to save Oji-chan's life. Still, gestures count.

The guys are on the field doing batting practice, but when we appear, Coach Jerry calls a time-out.

I hand the watermelon over to Tomomi and Maki, and they get busy serving pieces on paper plates, trying to keep everything civilized. Junji escorts Oji-chan to a canvas chair, and pretty soon he's sitting there with a slice of watermelon, pink juice dripping down his chin. Within minutes, he's surrounded by players. I figure he's telling some old-time baseball story. Maybe he's talking about his days on the mound, or the time he met Joe Dimaggio or the time his team went to Koshien.

At any rate, he looks like he fits right in.

It occurs to me that Oji-chan, who's always lived here, who's never gone abroad, is more of a part of this community than I am. These guys accept him as one of their own. He's like a tribal leader. I feel a little bit jealous at first. But then I realize that my grandfather is my connection to this place. And these guys? Maybe they're here now, but they might go away someday, too. But they'll always have this place to come back to.

During a pause in the storytelling, Mr. Jerry leans down next to me and says, "Hey, your grandfather knows a lot about baseball, doesn't he?" I think he would make a great assistant coach."

"Yeah..." Sounds like a plan. It would give him something to do, and I'd be able to keep a better eye on him. I'll have to talk it over with my parents, but I think it's a great idea. And maybe it would be more motivation to win, because who wants to see an old man cry? But before we get to all that, I have something to say. "Hey, guys? Thanks for helping find my grandfather. And, uh, I'm sorry about what happened during the last tournament. I should have paid attention to the coach. I know I should have bunted."

Some of the guys stare at me as if they are trying to judge my sincerity.

"Also, I'd like to do something for the team to help make amends."

"Oh, yeah? What would that be?" Shintaro asks. Since we're here more or less unofficially, Shintaro is once again unofficially on the team.

"Well, I know some of the guys aren't doing that well in English class," I begin, with a glance over at Shintaro. "I think I can help them. I'd like to set up an English study group for the baseball players and be their tutor."

His eyes narrow. Maybe he thinks I'm backing out on my promise to help him cheat. And yeah, I guess I am.

Mr. Jerry, on the other hand, starts clapping. "That is a great idea, Satoshi. Let's give it a try. We can start tomorrow after practice."

"Thank you, sir."

"Practice is at nine a.m.," he adds. "Wear your uniform."

I've missed these guys so much. I feel a burning behind my eyeballs. I don't trust myself to speak, so I just take a deep bow.

· · ·

When I arrive at the baseball field the next morning, it's like the summer tournament never happened. Or at least everyone seems to have forgiven me for how I lost the game. Shintaro shoves a rake into my hands. Oji-chan settles in a chair in the shade. Pretty soon I'm out on the clay, playing catch with Junji. After all those hours of just me and the batting center robots, this is a nice change.

We stretch and do windsprints, and then break up into two teams. Shintaro is pitching, and I'm third at bat. I can see that he's in total control of the ball. He's more focused than before, more confident. He's a regular now, and he has no reason to resent me.

Both guys ahead of me strike out.

When I step into the batter's box, he fixes me with a glare, trying to psyche me out. But when I hit the first pitch, smack it clear to the fence, he breaks into a grin. Maybe I'm reading too much into this, but it looks like he's happy to have me back.

Even though I hit that straight ball, I know that Shintaro is good. Maybe even as good as

Kikawa, our previous pitcher, and I know he can become better. This team could seriously win some games. I feel it in my gut. We could make it all the way to the national tournament, and then some. But for now, we've just got to make it to the final round of the fall regional tournament.

After practice, I get permission to use the club house for my after-game English tutoring session. There are no showers at school—one of the things I miss most about Atlanta—so I change from my sweaty practice uniform into a pair of shorts and a T-shirt.

34

At first, it's just me. I worry that no one will show up. But then Junji skulks in and takes a seat at the table. A couple of other guys, who are a year ahead of us in school, follow. Two more from a different homeroom stumble in. I smile.

"Okay, let's get started." I dig into my backpack and pull out a soft, squishy ball and hold it up for them to see. In one of my first ESL classes, we played an ice breaker game where we sat in a circle and each person had to tell about something that they liked. It seemed a little juvenile, but it just might work. Our brains are fried from being out in the hot sun anyway. It's not like we're ready to discuss the state of the world.

I pick up a piece of chalk and write an S on the board. "My name is Satoshi and I like spaghetti." Next, I toss the ball to Junji who catches it like a

Golden Glove athlete. I draw a J on the board.

He squirms a little. "My name is Junji, and I like, uh, juice."

The door squeaks open. Shintaro saunters in, just in time to hear Itsuki say that he likes ice cream. Our eyes meet and he nods slightly. He drops into a vacant seat. So, I guess I won't have to help him cheat after all.

Towards the end of the session, I look over to see Principal Mori standing in the doorway, listening in with a hint of a smile. I think he approves.

• • •

That evening, the doorbell rings. I look through the peephole and see Misa standing there.

"Hi!" She's smiling. "Here, I brought this for your grandfather." She hands me a white box. It's bigger than a cake box, much heavier, and it's moving.

I set it down and peek inside. There's a ball of blonde fur. Little flaps of ears. Brown eyes look up at me.

"It's a puppy!"

"I thought he might need it since Nana-chan is gone," Misa says. "Our moms have already talked about this. They thought it was a good idea, too. You can train him to help your grandfather with stuff."

The puppy makes a squeaky sound. His little tail beats against the side of the box. I reach in and rub his nose.

I can see it now: Oji-chan and this dog will become the best of friends. The dog will keep track of my grandfather with his super-sensitive snout and bark his head off if something is wrong. We can probably even teach him to bring slippers to guests. Maybe they can both come to baseball practice. I get this image of the dog in a Tokushima Whirlpool Junior High School doggie t-shirt, retrieving stray balls, bringing the school fame as its team mascot. Hey, it could happen.

"Let's take him over together," I say. "Oji-chan will be happy to see you."

"Misa-chan!" Oji-chan says as soon as we walk in the door. Good! He remembers!

She holds out the box to him. Before he can take it, the puppy pops its head out and starts licking his face. Oji-chan's eyes widen in surprise, but then he starts laughing. He reaches for the puppy and takes it into his arms. It's like an instant bond. Misa doesn't even have to tell him that the puppy is a gift for him.

"I think I'll call him Hachi," he says. His eyes are full of tears.

35

School starts back up the first week of September. There's no more time for post-practice English lessons in the clubhouse, but after we've finished putting away all of our gear and some of the players have started for home, Shintaro comes up to me.

"We have our first English test next week, right?" he says.

"Um, yeah..." Is he about to ask me to help him cheat? I know that he isn't exactly fluent in English, but he's made a lot of progress. He could probably squeak by and keep his place on the team.

He shuffles his feet, looks down at the ground, and up at me again. "Could you help me study some more this week?"

Between school and baseball and helping out at home, I don't have lots of time. Maybe he could get his parents to send him to cram school. I'm about to refuse, when I get an idea.

"Tomorrow," I say. "At lunch."

The next day, Shintaro follows me down the hall and up the stairs. I glance behind us to make sure no one sees where we're going. When we get to the Art room, I knock on the door although I know they're expecting me.

"What's going on?" Shintaro asks.

"Shhh. Let me handle this."

The door slides open. Shina's standing there. At the sight of Shintaro, her mouth drops open. She nervously adjusts her eye-patch.

"It's okay. He's with me," I say. "He wants to practice English."

For a moment, I think she's going to slide the door shut, but Mr. Jerry calls out, "Come on in! The more, the merrier."

I step into the room with Shintaro right behind me. Masaki freezes up, and Misa seems to shrink down into her seat. It reminds me of how they reacted the first time I came up here.

"I've got a favor to ask you all. Shintaro needs to pass the next English test or he'll get kicked off the baseball team. He's the best pitcher we have. If he can't pitch, we can't win. So, for the sake of our school, how about we all help him out?"

Shintaro bows deeply, at least pretending to be humble.

Everyone is shocked into silence. Jerry finally breaks the spell. He claps his hands together. "Okay, then, let's get started!"

"Thanks, Coach," Shintaro mumbles.

We spend about an hour quizzing him on vocabulary.

I'm impressed by how well he concentrates. He's made a lot of progress over the past few weeks. He cares about succeeding more than I thought he did.

As we head back to class. Shintaro leans in close and says, "Don't tell anyone about this, okay?" There's a hint of menace in his voice, but I can tell he's feeling embarrassed.

"I won't," I say, suddenly realizing that I can ask for something in return. "I'll keep my mouth shut under one condition."

He doesn't reply, but I can tell he's listening.

Finally, I work up the guts to add, "I'll keep it a secret if you stop being so hard on Misa."

"Okay, whatever," he mumbles. We walk back side by side.

· · ·

The air is still like soup—hot and heavy, but the screech of the cicadas has died down. We're allowed to wear short sleeves until October. I went to the barber shop yesterday and got another buzz cut, to show my devotion to our team, ready for the autumn tournament.

I wheel my bicycle to the bike shed, lock it up, and make my way to the entrance where we change our shoes.

When I walk into the classroom, Mr. Tanaka announces that he has created a new seating chart. I find my name and take my place. This time, I'm in the back, far away from Mr. Tanaka, which is kind of a relief, and Shintaro is in the front.

"I hope you all studied hard during summer vacation," Mr. Tanaka says. "Tomorrow we will have our first test."

A few students groan, even though they must have known this was coming.

Shintaro shoots a look of panic over his shoulder, but I give him the thumbs-up sign. He's going to do so much better than before, and since he's up front, Mr. Tanaka will know that he's not cheating.

"And now, open your books to page 44."

• • •

The next morning as Mr. Tanaka passes out our English tests, my hands are all sweaty from nerves—not for me, but for Shintaro. It's two weeks before the start of the autumn tournament. If Shintaro and the other guys doesn't pass this test, they won't be able to play and I will have failed my teammates again.

I breeze through mine in half an hour. When I've answered the last question, I sneak a glance across the room at Shintaro. He looks relaxed and confident. His pencil is flying across the page nonstop. I breathe a sigh of relief and put my head down on my desk.

36

Before the first game of the fall tournament begins, when we are all standing around about to discuss our game plan with Oji-chan and Mr. Jerry, I hand over a chain of origami cranes to be hung in the dugout for good luck. The birds are all different colors, all perfectly folded.

Oji-chan accepts the garland with a nod.

"Did you make them yourself?" Shintaro asks. I can tell he's not impressed, that he thinks it's a hobby for sissies.

"No, actually, my sister made them," I say. Misa helped, too, but Momoko did most of the work. She should get the credit.

Shintaro's sneer is replaced by an expression of shame. "Oh. Wow. Tell her thank you," he says. "And I'm sorry for what I said about her being, you know, a retard."

I shrug. "You should tell her yourself." I chop one hand against the back of my other hand, showing him the Japanese sign-language sign for "thank you."

He nods, and tries out the sign himself.

"Okay, guys, let's go!" Mr. Jerry a.k.a. Coach Jerry calls out, clapping his hands.

The moment is over. Some of us head for the stands. The rest file into the dugout or onto the diamond. I look up into the stands. I see Coach Ogawa. What's he doing here? Doesn't he have a new team to coach? Maybe it was just a rumor that he left for Kobe. Principal Mori is up there, too, wearing a baseball cap to shield his eyes from the sun. And hey, there's my dad and mom, and Misa and her parents.

When Shintaro takes the mound, I take my stance in right field. Before the first pitch, I yell out *"Ganbare, Nakamoto!"*

He winds up and slings the ball straight across the plate. The batter swings and misses. Next, he throws it inside. Strike two. The third ball is outside, but the batter swings anyway. Shintaro strikes out the first guy with only three pitches. *Yesssss! Atta boy!*

I see Oji-chan raise his fist in a salute. I feel proud. Of Shintaro. Of myself. And the team. I join in with the other guys to cheer. A roar goes out across the stadium. I imagine the sound going beyond, into the city, the country, into outer space. Although we are many individuals, it sounds like one big voice!

About the Author

Suzanne Kamata was born and raised in the United States, but she has lived in Tokushima Prefecture, Japan, for over half of her life. She earned an M.F.A. degree from the University of British Columbia. In addition to writing many stories, essays, and books, she has taught English as  a Foreign Language to learners of all ages. Suzanne raised two kids and knows all about baseball. She is married to a former Japanese high school baseball coach and is mother to a baseball player.

About the Illustrator

Tracy Nishimura Bishop grew up on a U.S. Army base in Japan from the age of 5 through 13 and got hooked on drawing when she won an art contest in Kindergarten. As a child, she loved reading Japanese manga.

Tracy attended San Jose State University and enrolled in the animation/ illustration program. She quickly discovered that she loved telling stories with illustrations and now works to tell great stories with her art.